Praise for *The Snake Charmer*

"The year's best fiction . . . A deft and intricate telling of a deceptively simple story about a snake charmer's search for solace on a path that leads from medicine to magic to sexual betrayal."
—*A. Magazine*

"Nigam spins an engaging, light-as-a-feather tale of a comically stubborn struggle for both moral absolution and a few dollops of worldly pleasure. . . . Sonalal is, in short, a marvelous creation, a captivating figure of both strangeness and recognizability."
—*The New York Times*

"Bids fair to join this select company [of Arundhati Roy and Vikram Chandra]. . . . In Sonalal, Nigam has been able to create a convincing character who, though lowly and of low caste, is able to aspire toward perfection and at least once in his life senses it. It is this achievement that makes *The Snake Charmer* an exceptional novel."
—*The Washington Post Book World*

"This literary debut by the multiply-gifted Dr. Nigam is a thoroughly engaging satire of the circular fates of men and snakes, rendered with nimble prose and tail delicately in cheek."
—*The Dallas Morning News*

"A novel of enchantments—altogether a good and entertaining read."
—Oscar Hijuelos, Pulitzer Prize-winning author of *Mambo Kings Play Songs of Love*

"This arresting and old-fashioned first novel is about fleeting renown, sex, betrayal, and, in the end, making do—which, as the author clearly knows, attends any life in art."
—*The New Yorker*

"The new face of fiction. . . . Nigam's skill, his love for tumbledown Old Delhi—where his grandparents used to live—and his sure eye and ear for Indian detail make his novel a fascinating hybrid. It is a timeless-feeling fable about art, love, and transcendence that is also spiced with the real: film, music, Sanjay Gandhi, and India's rush into the world economy."
—*Utne Reader*

"The midlife crisis of a Delhi snake charmer: This plotline alone proves that Indian literature is the freshest flavor on the knowing literary plate. And Sanjay Nigam's slim tale of disaster mixed with hilarity yielding hard-won wisdom will resound with many middle-aged readers—even those who do not wheedle cobras out of wicker baskets to entertain tourists for a living. The opening of *The Snake Charmer* qualifies as very possibly the season's best."
—*USA Today*

"Hard to resist . . . a sensuous and elegant story. Told with sensitivity and compassion, Sanjay Nigam's debut novel is a delight."
—*Redbook*

"An exquisite creation, elegant and funny and smart and sad, a remarkable story of great and strange happenings in the life of a poor artist, an apparently simple man who commits a crime against his art, and who, for a time, loses his way in life. A dignified, accomplished, wholly satisfying work. A world lives inside this book."
—Donald Antrim, author of *The Hundred Brothers*

"A small gem of a story that entertains, moves—and, naturally, charms."
—*Kirkus Reviews*

"*The Snake Charmer* encompasses sadness, acceptance and loss, but it also carries another theme. It is only right that man, however humble, should reach for the stars, but he also has to keep his feet on the ground. There has to be room in life for both spiritual and material concerns. It is a book written from the soul and makes for an intensely satisfying read."   —*San Francisco Chronicle*

"A stunning portrait of a man's lifelong battles with his demons."
—*Booklist*

"Of all the poor miscreants who have ever had reason to wail 'My whole life has been ruined by a single moment of stupidity,' no one has bellowed this pitiful confession with the same tragicomic flair as Sonalal, the dhoti-clad hero of Sanjay Nigam's charming debut novel. . . . Nigam rises to the occasion as artfully as Raju the cobra in this curry-flavored portrait of the artist as a middle-aged paanwala."
—*Detour* magazine

"*The Snake Charmer* is [a] heartfelt and intriguing modern-day fable about pride, perfection and discovery of love in unexpected places. . . . Nigam seems to have absorbed the sights, smells and sounds of the country, which he brings out in the book with vigorous drama and deep insights."   —*India Today*

PENGUIN BOOKS

THE SNAKE CHARMER

Sanjay Nigam is a physician and medical researcher. His work has appeared in *Story*, *Grand Street*, *The Kenyon Review*, and *Natural History*. He was chosen by *Utne Reader* as one of the ten writers "changing the face of American fiction." *The Snake Charmer* is his highly acclaimed first novel.

THE SNAKE CHARMER

A Novel

SANJAY NIGAM

PENGUIN BOOKS

PENGUIN BOOKS
Published by the Penguin Group
Penguin Putnam Inc., 375 Hudson Street,
New York, New York 10014, U.S.A.
Penguin Books Ltd, 27 Wrights Lane,
London W8 5TZ, England
Penguin Books Australia Ltd, Ringwood,
Victoria, Australia
Penguin Books Canada Ltd, 10 Alcorn Avenue,
Toronto, Ontario, Canada M4V 3B2
Penguin Books (N.Z.) Ltd, 182–190 Wairau Road,
Auckland 10, New Zealand

Penguin Books Ltd, Registered Offices:
Harmondsworth, Middlesex, England

First published in the United States of America by
William Morrow and Company, 1998
Reprinted by arrangement with William Morrow and Company, Inc.
Published in Penguin Books 1999

3   5   7   9   10   8   6   4   2

Interior illustrations by Neil Brennan

The Snake Charmer is based on a short story that first appeared in *Grand Street.*

THE LIBRARY OF CONGRESS HAS CATALOGED THE HARDCOVER EDITION AS FOLLOWS:
Nigam, Sanjay.
The snake charmer: a novel/Sanjay Nigam.
p.   cm.
ISBN 0-688-15809-9 (hc.)
ISBN 0 14 02.7891 5 (pbk.)
I. Title.
PR9499.3.N48S63   1998
813'.54—dc21   97–49339

Printed in the United States of America
Set in Berkeley Book
Designed by Kathleen Flanigan

FOR V, WITH MUCH LOVE

But look! What was that?
One of the snakes had seized hold of its own tail,
and the form whirled mockingly before my eyes!

—FRIEDRICH AUGUST KEKULE, 1890

THE SNAKE CHARMER

1

SOME LIFETIMES seem to hinge on a single day, and for Sonalal today was that day. Even though he had no idea what lay in store when he woke up in the morning, like everyone else in the city, he was excited. The Games were opening today, and most of Delhi had declared an unofficial holiday. But not Sonalal. With so many foreign tourists in the city for the next two weeks, he could not pass up the chance to make a lot of money from just a little extra work.

Sonalal rolled out of bed, stood up, and stretched his arms. Though average height for his village, he was short by city standards. Countless hours in the sun had made his skin creased beyond his years. He had the kind of face seen in newsmagazine photographs of the faceless masses. So faceless did he sometimes appear that his wife, Sarita, had trouble finding him in crowds—which now and then proved quite convenient. But while Sonalal's face was not striking, his hands were. He had long, thin, double-jointed fingers that made exquisite music on his *been*. Some said he was the best charmer in all India.

After dressing, he went to the corner of the room and picked up his new *been,* which he had recently fashioned from a dried-out pumpkin. He ran his fingers over the instrument's smooth surface, wondering if it needed more fine tuning. But he was eager to try it out before an audience. Without further debate, he slipped the new instrument into a burlap bag containing his turban. Then he dragged out a wicker basket from underneath his cot.

"Wake up, Raju *beta*! It's time to go."

A slithering sound came from inside the basket. Sonalal lifted the top off and gently ran his forefinger over the markings on the cobra's hood. He kissed Raju twice on the nose, then stroked him some more. The temperamental snake remained stiff, but Sonalal could tell that Raju was enjoying the attention. At last Sonalal put the top back over the basket. As he headed for the door, he shouted a perfunctory good-bye to Sarita, who was still in the bathroom. He was outside before she could ask what time he'd be home.

His two sons were practicing field hockey shots with the bank clerk's son in the courtyard next door. A satisfied smile crept across Sonalal's face as he watched his sons. Who would have guessed the boys' parents had once been starving villagers? The family had come a long way, though unlike the bank clerk next door, Sonalal rented old servant quarters. The family was lucky to afford even that tiny space. While they lived in a very modest locality, such lodgings would ordinarily have been well beyond their means. But Sarita, expert negotiator that she was, had haggled the rent down to almost nothing by promising to do some chores and take care of the place while the owner, a retired army captain, escaped to his son's house in Jammu during the summer heat. Even though Sonalal and family were neither quite tenants nor servants, the captain, a quiet widower, didn't exploit their ambiguous position and mostly left them alone.

Sonalal waved to his sons, who did not notice him. Then he

opened the wrought-iron gate and headed for the bus stop. The day was already warming up. Sonalal overtook a thin cow as it lazily sauntered down the unpaved road, swatting flies with its tail. At the corner, a roadside barber lathered up someone for a shave. Sonalal walked past the local market, where the shutters of shops were down this morning, the only activity being in front of the vegetable stand.

Though the bus stop was less than a kilometer away, the weight of the wicker basket and burlap bag made it seem much farther. Just when Sonalal was within view of the stop, he saw a bus leave. He sighed. The next bus didn't come for another twenty minutes. By then, a line had formed. But Sonalal was up front and so the first on board. That always worked out best, for it allowed time to settle into a rear seat before others crammed in. Rarely did people suspect he carried a cobra in his basket. Even when they did, they seemed to prefer not knowing for certain; they usually just moved to different seats or stood until their stops came. Unfortunately, every now and then someone became hysterical or even screamed. Explaining that his cobra had been defanged and that the venom glands had been extracted made little difference: Some people simply refused to ride buses with snakes. Inevitably, the conductor would feel compelled to kick Sonalal off. But conductors treated him with much more courtesy than others they kicked off who didn't carry cobras.

While Sonalal sat in front of Humayun's Tomb waiting for tourists, sweat weighing down his lavender turban, dust reddening his eyes, he passed time conversing with his cobra. He and Raju had been together some fifteen years, and no charmer ever loved his snake as much as Sonalal did. Several years ago, the two had entered midlife together, comforting each other through its many tribulations. But while Sonalal could still claim to be middle-aged, Raju had become old, at least by snake standards. And yet, Sonalal continued to think of Raju as a son—his eldest and his favorite.

Raju had lots of personality, even for a cobra, and an hour went by just like that. The two were still chatting away when the first tourist bus rumbled in, followed by a trail of black exhaust nearly twice the length of the bus itself.

"Back inside!" said Sonalal. "Quick, Raju, quick!"

Sonalal placed the cover over Raju's basket, then took out his new *been* and waited for the approaching tourist bus. As soon as the bus came to a halt, he jumped aboard. Up and down the aisle he walked, playing eerie music on his *been*, the wicker basket containing Raju slung over his shoulder. Sonalal was delighted by the sound of his new *been*. When he felt he'd aroused enough interest on the bus, he hopped off, set the basket on the ground, and began to charm Raju.

With a mischievous glint in his eyes, the snake rose, swaying from side to side with yogic grace, not following the movements of the *been* as other cobras do, but anticipating them—guiding them. Old age had made Raju irritable and lazy, but when he danced it was with the energy and suppleness of a much younger snake. He often teased Sonalal with moves so unexpected, so complex, only an old master could have conceived them. Sonalal always did his best to match his tune and rhythm to Raju's mood, but most of the time he wasn't sure who was charming whom.

As Raju's dance grew livelier, more and more tourists crowded around, chattering in different languages, snapping photo after photo. Sonalal actually had mixed feelings about all this. While he saw himself as an artist, he knew tourists didn't view him that way. Soon they'd leave India on the same huge planes they came in, for Japan or England or America, where they'd show their friends the photos they were now taking alongside ones of dancing monkeys and street freaks. This was the price of earning a living, and some days it seemed too high. Then again, how many people make a living doing what they love most?

Up front in this morning's crowd was a family of foreign Indians. Sonalal wished they'd move away, since foreign Indians tended to be more tightfisted than Europeans and Japanese. Almost always, they watched a while, bringing their children in close, then left without giving any money.

But today was different. At the end of Sonalal's performance, a foreign Indian boy of ten or eleven turned to his father and said in broken Hindi, "Can I give some money to the charmer?"

The father grudgingly handed the boy a rupee, saying, "This is nothing—you see it all over India."

That was too much for Sonalal. He stood up and yelled, "Keep your money! You can't see a *tamasha* like mine anywhere in India. Nowhere! There is only one place in the whole world where you can see a performance of this quality, and that's right here. So you're very lucky—at least if you know how to tell art from cheap tricks."

The boy's father just laughed.

Sonalal's face became twisted from anger. "Get back on your air-conditioned tourist bus!" he shouted. "Go back to America or wherever you came from—traitors to your motherland!"

"He's a madman," the boy's father muttered as he whisked his family away.

Much to Sonalal's chagrin, his outburst also chased away the other tourists, some of whom looked rich and might have tipped him well—if he'd kept his composure. So he ended up giving that performance for free. Dejected and already tired, he returned to his spot and waited for the next bus, hoping the day would pass quickly.

The take from the next tourist bus more than made up for the first, and in no time there was a constant flow of buses packed with foreign tourists in town for the Games. Sonalal's pockets were bulging with coins and rupees after just two hours of charming. For once, he felt appropriately compensated for his talent. These foreigners might not know the sweet song of a nightingale from the blaring horn of a truck, but then how many Indians did? All these years, he'd been playing the finest music in the land. Who cared?

The buses kept coming. Sonalal gave one performance after another, Raju dancing almost continuously. By the end of the afternoon, Sonalal saw that Raju's moves were getting sluggish. He too was ready to call it a day. After charming for nine hours straight, his pockets were stuffed with rupees and jingling with loose change, and he feared someone might rob him while he made his way home. Delhi wasn't as safe as it used to be. On the other hand, for a man with a cobra, it seemed safe enough for another hour or so. He lingered.

Dusk was approaching, and along came yet another bus, this one full of foreign journalists covering the Games. Sonalal almost passed it up. But then he thought: This bus is for me. After all, he'd already done his duty to his family. In a single day, he'd made enough to take care of more than one month's expenses. He deserved this bus. Specifically, he had in mind a special liquor he'd once caught a whiff of but could never afford. Now he could almost taste its bitter sting. So, as the bus slowed down, Sonalal jumped aboard with his basket and piped his tune while walking up and down the aisle, just as he'd done two dozen times earlier in the day. Then he jumped off the bus and tossed his basket on the ground. The cover of the basket rolled away, and he started to charm Raju.

Sonalal played and played, but the old cobra wouldn't come out. Raju was spoiled and lazy to begin with and now, after such a long day, exhausted. Sonalal understood. He was tired too. Tomorrow he'd take the day off. And, if he made enough from this bus, in the evening he'd go out for that special liquor; Raju might also enjoy a few sips.

"One last time," Sonalal said lovingly to Raju, and played the cobra's favorite tune.

Raju's head slowly rose out of the basket. A cheer erupted from the crowd of foreign journalists. But the tired cobra couldn't rise any further. With a vacant expression, Raju sank back into his basket.

Sonalal was acutely embarrassed. His glistening brown face reddened. Here he was, the best charmer in the land, yet in front of all these people from around the world, he couldn't even get his snake to come out of its basket! This had never happened before. And at that moment, he felt as if these foreigners had come from faraway places not to see the Games, but to witness his performance. He *had* to make Raju dance!

So Sonalal began to play variations on Raju's favorite tune, such beautiful variations that, had they been recorded, might have guaranteed Sonalal's immortality. It was as if the finest music of his ancestors—seven generations of charmers—had condensed into the enchanting combination of notes now coming from his new *been*.

If anyone had a more discriminating ear than Sonalal, it was Raju. And though extremely tired, the snake couldn't resist music so beautiful. As if in a trance, Raju rose out of his basket, swaying from side to side with the music. In no time, the snake was dancing with great verve and grace, almost levitating. Sonalal was enraptured—over his music and Raju's dancing. He'd never seen a cobra dance so magnificently in all his forty-four years!

The thrilled journalists flashed their cameras, shouting encouragement. Newly arrived in India, they rewarded Sonalal according to Western standards—at the airport exchange rate. Sonalal was delighted by the sight of so much money. Five-, ten-, twenty-, even hundred-rupee notes flew at him and Raju, amid a shower of clanging coins, which heightened the effect of his music.

Sonalal was so excited he hit a false note. None of the journalists noticed the error: The cheering, the flashes, the Monsoon of money, kept on. But Raju suddenly stopped dancing. The cobra fell to the ground, curled up.

Sonalal knelt down and whispered, "Get up, Raju. It's almost over."

The snake didn't move a scale.

"Raju!"

All of a sudden, the snake rose on end, hissing menacingly, hood spread, eyes blazing. The journalists fell silent. In all their years together, Sonalal had never seen Raju act this way.

Sonalal circled Raju. Once, twice, three times, he made his way completely around the furious cobra.

"Don't worry, Raju *beta*," he said. "Everything will be fine. We're done now. Let's just go home."

The rage didn't leave Raju's eyes. Sonalal began to sweat. He didn't know this snake anymore.

Carefully, Sonalal stepped back. He was about to take another step back when Raju shot out and bit his left calf.

The crowd gasped. Since Sonalal had removed Raju's fangs and venom glands, he had no fear of serious injury. But Raju had never tried to bite him. Never!

Someone was getting a taxi to take Sonalal to the hospital. Raju lay stretched out on the ground, pale and motionless, completely spent—almost dead. Seeing that Raju had put everything into his malevolent lunge only fueled Sonalal's anger. He gazed at his cobra like a father irremediably wronged by his son. Raju looked back timidly.

Sonalal felt no pity. His eyes became wild. He bent down, grabbed the listless snake by the head and tail, and stretched it to its full length. Then he closed his eyes, growled, and opened his mouth wide. All Sonalal's rage concentrated in his jaws.

He bit.

Two wriggling cobra halves fell and squirmed on the ground. Then they became still.

Sonalal gazed up at the evening sky, his face dripping with bitter snake juice, and cried over the death of his eldest son.

2

THE JOURNALISTS rushed over, snapping more photos. Sonalal just kept crying. When his tears stopped for a moment, the journalists fired questions, which the tour guide translated. Still shocked at what he'd done, Sonalal couldn't answer.

A taxi finally arrived, and the journalists insisted Sonalal go to the hospital.

"There is no need," he muttered. "My cobra had no poison in him."

"Are you sure?" asked the tour guide.

"I'm sure."

Someone gathered the money that had been tossed during the performance—over three thousand rupees—and presented the sum to Sonalal. He wouldn't touch it, the money of child slaughter.

The journalists whispered among themselves, fished into their pockets, passed more money around. A white woman journalist with red hair offered Sonalal the stack, now over nine thousand rupees.

Sonalal shook his head.

The tour guide came up and put his arm over Sonalal's shoulder. "Take it, *dost*. They're trying to help you. And you'll need it. You've lost your livelihood. Do you have a family?"

Sonalal nodded.

"Then you must take it."

After some more urging, Sonalal accepted the money.

Three hours later, the last of the journalists left. They'd been relentless in their inquiries, and once Sonalal began to answer, the questions multiplied.

All the attention had the effect of making Sonalal feel remote from the butchery, as if someone else had committed the murder and he was just a key witness. Now alone, he was horrified by what he'd done. He had killed his own son—spilled his own blood! Could there be anyone baser than he? He deserved to be whipped unconscious, then hanged. Or shot in the head.

Sonalal's jaws suddenly began to ache as though they had been clobbered by a hammer. A bitter taste overwhelmed his mouth. He stood in one place, unable to move. A part of him seemed to leave his body and view the scene from far away. He felt drunk, but with none of the levity of drunkenness.

Taking small steps, he slowly made his way back to the spot of the killing. For nearly an hour, he stared at the two halves of Raju. At last he picked up the pieces and put them in the basket, joining them as best he could. In vain he hoped for a miracle that would reverse everything.

"What have I done?" he said over and over as he stood still in the warm night.

He went back to the basket, knelt. Tears streamed down his

cheeks. He kissed each half of Raju, begged forgiveness for his sin. Then he placed a hundred and one rupees inside the basket and covered it. Still kneeling, he clasped his hands, closed his eyes, and prayed. "O God," he said in a quavering voice, "punish me however you wish, but bring my Raju back."

He opened his eyes and looked up at the heavens, as if expecting an answer. But there was none. Nothing could make up for what he'd done.

He sat alone in the dark, past the time when the homeless crept into the tomb to sleep till dawn. Numb and woozy, he gazed up at the night sky. It was a moonless night. He would have done just about anything for a moon.

His uncle used to say a man must burn any snake he kills, for otherwise whomever the snake sees before dying becomes etched in the eyes of its ghost, and the ghost then tracks its killer. Sonalal considered this no more than a superstition. But it reminded him of something about which there could be no doubt: If a cobra is killed, its mate will not rest until it gets revenge.

A shudder passed through Sonalal's whole body.

He set the basket on fire around midnight. The flames licked up the night and threw long slender shadows against the outer walls of the tomb. It was as though the burning dead snake had given rise to hundreds of new snakes, each dancing wildly to a different tune. Sonalal watched his beloved Raju turn to smoke. Eventually, only sparks and ashes remained. He watched every spark die out, then sat motionless in absolute darkness.

It was a long time before he moved again. Still sitting, he grabbed the edge of his *dhoti* and ripped out a piece. He uttered a solemn prayer for Raju and then, with great care, scooped the snake's ashes off the ground. He wrapped them in the cloth and knotted it.

Tormented by sorrow and guilt, he wandered through the streets around the tomb. In the flicker of streetlamps, the dry trees lining the roads resembled skeletons. Gradually his grief turned into anger. He began to rant. How could Raju have attacked him? Raju, his son! Should a man just take it when his own son rises up against him? And for what? Playing one wrong note—just one!—and that too after playing so many beautiful notes! How could Raju, whom he had raised and always doted on—often to the neglect of his human sons—have acted like that?

Suddenly he felt ashamed for having such base thoughts. It was he who'd committed the crime. Such an enormous sin! "Oh, my poor son!" he cried out loud. Then he wept all over again.

He wanted to kill himself. He went up to a tree, stood with the back of his head just inches from the trunk. Then he shut his eyes and banged his head against the bark. It didn't hurt enough. So he banged his head harder. And again, even harder. He swayed for a moment, moaning from the tremendous pain, then fell to the ground.

He regained consciousness ten minutes later. His head felt like firecrackers were exploding inside, one after another. He got up and staggered down the street—groaning, sobbing, ranting. A constable stopped him.

"What city are you in?" asked the constable.

"Delhi."

"How many stars are in the sky?"

"More than hairs on your head."

Evidently satisfied Sonalal wasn't drunk or insane, the constable then asked, "Why are you roaming outside in the middle of the night?"

"I'm returning from the cremation of my son."

The constable looked suspicious. "So late? Hmm . . . Well, I'm sorry. And be careful. We are on the watch tonight because of the Games. There could be trouble."

"Trouble?"

"Yes, yes, trouble. Just go home."

It was one of those rare moments when going home seemed a good idea. But there was one final matter.

Sonalal watched the constable walk away until he was no longer visible. He waited a few more minutes, just to be sure. Then he pulled his new *been* out of the burlap bag. As he stared at the wicked instrument that piped the music of death, he shook his head slowly. He then raised the *been* high and hurled it down on the ground as hard as he could. Again and again he hurled the *been,* grunting louder each time, till the sound at contact changed, and he knew the loathsome instrument had cracked. The second and third cracks came easier. Then he stomped on the shattered *been* until his feet hurt.

He was ready to go home.

3

"WHERE HAVE you been?" his wife asked as soon as Sonalal stepped inside.

He was used to Sarita's accusatory tone. Quite often she had good reason to accuse. She also had an uncanny ability to almost guess what he'd been up to. But almost was almost, and her mistakes rarely worked in his favor. So sure was she of her ability to read his mind that sometimes she just stared at him with intense concentration like a clairvoyant and responded to his thoughts as if he'd voiced them in the first place. But of course, today it was impossible for her to guess what had happened.

"Were you drinking?" she asked.

She sniffed his breath before he could answer.

"Or have you been to the brothel?"

He shook his head. The shaking caused a horrible pain in every part of his head. He winced, then rubbed the spot on his scalp that he'd banged against the tree.

She examined his face. He had a lazy left eye, which became even lazier when he was nervous, creating a sly look. He knew that was exactly what was happening right now, though he felt it wisest not to glance away. But he also didn't have the courage to peer straight into

Sarita's eyes. So he focused on the furrows of her brow, which at that moment resembled ravines.

Unable to come to any conclusion from Sonalal's face, Sarita scanned the rest of his body for additional clues. She carefully inspected his *dhoti*, which wasn't tied very neatly. "Aha!" she said, pointing to where he'd ripped out the piece of cloth to wrap up Raju's ashes. "Again I've caught you lying!"

"Listen, just listen!" he protested, glancing at the boys' door.

"I'll listen. And don't worry, the children are asleep. What do you care? Such a useless father you are! Such a useless man! What is the story this time, Sona?"

In his self-deprecating mood, he pitied her. She's right, he thought. She is a good mother, living only for her children. And I am an irresponsible father, an even worse husband. So what, if she is wrong today?

"You won't believe this, Sarita."

"I'm sure I won't."

He wondered if he should just tell her outright. But no, then she wouldn't even try to understand. He had to explain everything from the start.

"It's so strange," he said.

"Get on with it!"

Slowly, bit by bit, he recounted the events of the evening. When he got to Raju's amazing dance, he couldn't help mentioning the beautiful music he'd played. "I never knew I was capable of making such music. Sarita, I felt like the gods were listening to my *been*! I felt like my music brought tears of joy to their eyes!"

"Go on."

When at last he got to his confrontation with Raju, his face began to twitch. He spoke so fast the words ran together.

"Slow down!"

He closed his eyes, took deep breaths in a vain attempt to settle himself. Then he continued, concentrating on the pause after each word.

Her eyes narrowed. "Raju bit you? My God! For all his moodiness, I've never seen that snake attack anyone!"

His voice became thready. "There's more."

"More? Where is Raju, anyway?"

He went into an uncontrollable fit of blinking. He had to look away.

"Look at me!"

He looked, tears in his eyes.

"Where's Raju?"

"Sarita, I've committed a terrible crime. An unforgivable sin!"

"What happened?"

"The worst thing I could have done!"

"What!"

Haltingly—with words that filled him with new horror—he told her.

She gasped as he stuttered out the gruesome details, each a spear piercing his chest.

"You bit our snake in two?" she shrieked.

His hands began to tremble. His face felt like it was burning up, every bone in his body as though it was melting. In a choked voice he said, "How I wish I could undo it all!"

Sarita wasn't listening. "You murdered Raju? How could you?

Such a great sin! Raju! Our Raju! You killed him—and like that! Are you crazy? Of course you are—I've always known it. Now you've gone too far, Sona. Too far! Raju is dead—that's horrible enough. But he was our livelihood. Life is already so tough. How will we survive now? And what about the children? I'm amazed they grow at all with so little milk. And how will we pay for their school books? Every year the price goes up. Soon they'll need another set of clothes too—Ramesh's socks are as thin as the thread I use to sew up their holes. And who will pay the rent? Oh, it's all lost! Everything! Captain *sahib* is a nice man, and I don't mind having to do a few chores for him—but now I will have to work for the neighbors, listen to the abuse of their children, clean their dirty dishes, wash their filthy clothes. Or we'll have to return to that shack in the trans-Jamuna slums, be at the mercy of thugs and thieves. Worse, go back to our village and starve! Don't you remember what it was like during the drought? When we left the village, all we had was the dirt beneath our fingernails. Have we gone through everything just to end up like that again? Sona, you did a terrible thing. It would have been better if you had come home from the brothel, drunk as usual. Or maybe you did that too! Let me see your face again."

Still trembling, he pulled a wad of money out of his pocket. Sarita snatched the money, stepped back. Then he took out more money from another pocket.

"Oh, my!"

Sonalal felt relieved to be unburdened of some of the sinful money, and now he wanted to be rid of it all. So he undid his *dhoti,* releasing dozens and dozens of rupee notes in all denominations. Then he dumped more than a kilogram of loose change out of the burlap bag. The coins clinked as they hit the floor, then rolled all over the room.

Sarita got on her knees. She was a bulky woman who could not be budged, physically or otherwise. As she slowly crawled across the cracked cement floor, picking up one coin at a time, Sonalal was reminded of a bus caught in rush hour traffic. Sarita's eyes, once large and gentle, had grown severe with time, but now when she glanced up at him, a little of the old softness had returned.

"So much!" she gasped, then went back to collecting the coins.

When she finally had all the money in one pile, she began to count it with great concentration. At some point, she seemed to have difficulty keeping track, and he wondered if she knew how to count that high. Now wasn't the time to ask. But she surmounted whatever problem there was and kept counting. He just stood there half naked, like a convicted prisoner waiting to learn whether he is going to spend the rest of his life chipping away at a granite mountain or be hanged. "My poor, poor Raju," he kept saying to himself. His whole body quaked with guilt and remorse. He felt so sick in the heart, so utterly worthless, he would have marched straight to the gallows had Sarita so ordered him.

Three quarters of an hour later, Sarita stuffed all the money into a large clay pot. Sonalal knew the money wouldn't stay there long. Soon it would be dispersed into the half-dozen or so hiding places she had around the house, the locations of which she kept changing in order to limit what he spent on his vices.

Sarita covered the pot full of money with a plate. Then she stared at Sonalal for a long while. He had no idea what was going through her head.

Eventually she spoke. "Sona, don't keep standing naked like that. Put your *dhoti* back on. You're no handsome film hero!"

But her tone was playful. And the way she smiled, he feared she had something else on her mind. He started to dress right away.

While wrapping his *dhoti,* he asked, "What do you think?"

"About what? There are so many things to think about."

"All of it."

She was silent a while. Then she said, "I will miss Raju dearly. Of course, he was so, so old. Better to go quickly than linger on."

4

BY MORNING, Sonalal was famous. His photograph was on the front page of almost every newspaper in the country. It had been an otherwise boring day in the world, and Sonalal's exploits were also reported in Rio, Istanbul, Brussels, Kinshasa, Manila, New York, Port-of-Spain, Hanga Roa, and other faraway places. In one Bombay newspaper, side by side with the caption "Games Begin," another caption said, "Snake Charmer Bites Cobra Back." The first paragraph of the article read:

> Outside the tomb of the Moghul emperor Humayun, father of Akbar the Great, a cobra bit a snake charmer yesterday evening while he was performing before a crowd. Undaunted, the charmer, one Mr. Sonalal, attacked the hissing creature back. A terrible battle ensued, the cobra up on its tail, lunging and lashing at the fearless man, who, like an acrobat, dodged each poisonous thrust. Eventually, Mr. Sonalal caught the undulating cobra by its ends and bit the creature in half. Mr. Sonalal said he was not afraid of the snake's venom and, even upon the insistence of the crowd, refused to see a doctor.

When he awoke, Sonalal knew nothing of his world renown. Although he liked looking at pictures in the newspaper, since he could neither read nor afford it, he didn't subscribe. And while fascinated by the incident, those of his neighbors who read the morning paper didn't pay attention to the charmer's face or name. Or if they did, they didn't link it to the uncommonly common man down the street who had the gall to rent lodgings in their neighborhood, even if they were old servant quarters.

While Sonalal still lay in bed that morning, he was preoccupied by the dream he'd had just before dawn. He'd dreamed the old Raju had turned into younger twin Rajus. At first he was overjoyed, but then he remembered what had really happened. Once again, he was overcome by the sheer horror of his crime. He pulled his hair as hard as he could, until tears were coursing down his face and he was ready to howl from the pain. He stopped. His head began to throb. How could he have murdered his beloved Raju? Innocent Raju! Sarita was right: Raju may have had a short temper, but he would never have attacked under ordinary circumstances. It was wicked to have made Raju dance that much. Evil! Raju was so old; all that dancing must have been awfully hard on him. Sonalal's own bones often ached in the morning, and some nights his back hurt so much he had to lie on the cement floor. And snakes have so many bones—all in their backs! Raju's bones must have been aching horribly when he forced the poor snake to dance that last time. No wonder Raju didn't want to come out of his basket.

Why did he push Raju so hard? Why? Why?

Greed. Only greed—that glass of special liquor.

But why couldn't he have just forgiven Raju? It was a harmless bite. Where had all his anger come from? His wrath! Venom may not have entered his blood, but it had certainly invaded his soul. He'd completely lost control. Such a terrible sin! And now, all that was left of poor Raju was his ashes and some old sloughed snakeskins. New tears streamed from Sonalal's eyes and wet the bedsheet. He sobbed quietly. He deserved the most severe, most painful punishment. Death!

But no, he wouldn't be punished. For Raju was a wild creature nobody cared about. Just look how Sarita had all but dismissed Raju's death last night. Surrounded by all those rupees, she forgot fifteen years of Raju's devotion just like that. Now that Sonalal thought about it, Sarita had always been jealous of his closeness to Raju. In an argument just last week, she had accused him of preferring Raju to his own sons. She was right, but contempt still filled him. Where was she anyway?

Right then, Sarita walked in, smiling affectionately, a cup of hot tea in her hands. Sonalal couldn't recall the last time she'd brought him tea in bed. He accepted the cup without a word.

She noticed his moist eyes. "Are you all right?"

He nodded.

"Are you sure?"

"Yes!"

She looked concerned but went away.

Slowly, he sipped. The hot tea soothed his anguish, calmed him. But then he imagined Raju crawling under the bedsheet, making his way to the cup for a few sips of tea, his favorite drink. Sonalal's hand shook. He set the cup down and closed his eyes.

He was startled by a loud knock at the door. Sarita answered. A minute later, she poked her head into the room. "It's a man from the newspaper," she said.

"Tell him to go."

Sarita looked disappointed. "I can't say that. I've already told him you're here."

"All right, let me dress."

He took his own time wrapping himself in a clean *dhoti*, then finally came out.

"Can I ask you some questions?" said the journalist, a dark man with glasses and short hair.

Sonalal tilted his head and sat back. "Go ahead."

As soon as the journalist took out his pen and note pad, again there was a knock at the door: another journalist. And within five minutes, two more.

After that, Sarita just left the door open. Soon the tiny room was crammed with journalists. Since most of Sonalal's earnings went to food and rent, the family owned little more than when they'd lived in the slums, and there was almost nowhere to seat the journalists. So some sat on the floor, while others stood leaning against unpainted walls. All these journalists were Indian, eager to glean what remained of the big story after having been scooped by their foreign counterparts in their own territory. They asked Sonalal to rehash the events of last night. At first he wasn't able to. "Oh, how I wish I'd stayed home yesterday like most working people!" he said. "Then none of this would have happened."

But the journalists coaxed the story out of him. And they were so responsive to his every word that he began to take liberties, embellishing the account. That helped in a way, for it began to seem like a bizarre story about some other charmer, some other snake. And because his sons were listening, he succumbed to the temptation of allowing his craven act to sound a bit heroic. After he finished, a pretty female journalist asked, "Don't you fear anything?"

Suddenly Sonalal felt like not only a murderer, but also a liar and a hypocrite. As he stared at the pretty journalist awaiting his answer, he realized he feared more things than most men. But he mentioned only the fear foremost in his mind. "Raju's mate."

"His mate?"

"If you kill a cobra," he said in a faint voice, "the cobra's mate seeks revenge."

Most of the journalists nodded solemnly, but one, a young man in jeans, seemed to think it was a joke.

Sonalal shook his finger at the smiling journalist. "It's true! There is no doubt about this. Raju's mate will get me."

The journalist stopped smiling.

"But Raju was very old," said Sonalal, "and so must be his mate. She may even be dead already. If she isn't, she knows what happened. She must be mourning, poor creature. I hope she knows how much I loved Raju—how much I grieve for him. Maybe she will pity me if she knows that. Raju came from hills far away. You have to take a long bus ride. Then, finally, you arrive near my ancestral village. From there, you have to go by foot to get to the hill where I found Raju. Such an old cobra—as Raju's mate must be—couldn't survive the journey from there to Delhi. Raju certainly couldn't. And then there is all the traffic in the city. Even cobras are nothing against mad truck drivers. No, it would be very hard for her to find me."

"But what if another charmer caught Raju's mate and brought her to Delhi?" asked the pretty journalist.

Sonalal swallowed nervously but didn't answer.

Now other journalists joined in, firing question upon question. They inquired about Sonalal's ancestors, his village, many other things. It was the first time educated people had asked for his opinions, and he replied thoughtfully.

A man with thin eyebrows wanted to know who his favorite film actresses were.

"I used to like Suraiya and Madhubala," said Sonalal. "These days, all actresses try to look like foreign women—bodies like sticks, funny hairstyles, ridiculous dresses. But I am not a foreign man, so why should I want to look at foreign women?"

An older journalist, a small man who reminded Sonalal of Lal Bahadur Shastri, then asked, "Do you believe some good will come out of the current political chaos, or are you simply disgusted like most people?"

It seemed an important question, and Sonalal took time to frame his reply. "Some politicians are rascals," he finally said. "But some really care. Unfortunately, it's impossible to tell one from the other. Maybe what India needs is a rascal who really cares."

Which led the older journalist to follow up with "What did you think of Sanjay Gandhi and the Emergency?"

Sonalal hadn't thought about Sanjay Gandhi in years. During the State of Emergency, he'd once taken a wrong turn in Old Delhi and been pulled into a sterilization tent, where he was offered a transistor radio. As much as he wanted a radio, he wasn't about to barter his precious manhood for anything. The trouble was that the people in the sterilization tent didn't seem to understand. They got rough with him. He took the blows, while valiantly protecting his prize. But when he told Sarita of his heroics, she said he always made the wrong decisions in life and should have taken the radio. Was he planning to have more children? With whom? Two were enough for her—she had no idea how many he had. Did he? Besides, a man who was as useless a father as he should be sterilized on principle. Because of all the aggravation, he voted against the government in the next election. But that had been long ago. And Delhi was so congested these days. Maybe sterilization wasn't such a bad idea—as long as he was spared.

"Well?" said the older journalist.

"Had he not died in that plane crash," said Sonalal, "Sanjay Gandhi might have been exactly the leader we now need."

As the journalists copied down his words on their note pads, Sarita rolled her eyes, much to Sonalal's vexation.

At last the journalists asked about a subject Sonalal could address with genuine authority: poisonous snakes. He spoke like a professor of herpetology. "You mainly have to worry about cobras, kraits, and vipers. At night, they hunt for rats and frogs, but if they find you, they can steal your last breaths as you sleep."

Their interest piqued, the journalists now began to ask very specific questions. They wanted to know how many eggs were in a viper's nest, how much venom a cobra produced in a day, what the life-span of a krait was. They wanted details, quantitative facts. Sonalal couldn't provide them. He began to feel foolish before all these educated people, and the amused look on Sarita's face didn't help matters. When asked how thick a king cobra was, he held out his hand and replied, "Thicker than my wrist."

That wasn't precise enough for the journalists. Frustrated, someone measured his wrist.

"One can know snakes as well as the gods who make them,"

Sonalal protested, "and still not know the kinds of things you want to know."

The journalists looked unimpressed, and several made motions as if they were ready to leave. But then somebody asked whether snakes were good or evil, a topic on which Sonalal was well informed.

"People misunderstand snakes," he said. "On the whole they are good, gentle creatures. Most will not harm you unless you threaten them. And not only are they very smart, they can be nobler than the noblest people. I see that you don't believe me, but snakes have often come to the aid of people, *rishis,* and even gods. Of course, there are a few dangerous snakes too. The Great Snake Demon lives in the underworld. Each of his nine hoods is studded with diamonds, rubies, and emeralds, and he guards a treasure more valuable than the Peacock Throne. My mother once told me . . ."

And so, Sonalal went on and on, recounting just about every story his parents, grandparents, aunts, and uncles had told him, stories he hadn't thought about in many years. The stories fused his past and present, warmed his heart. At some point, the journalists stopped taking notes and just listened. Even Sarita seemed engrossed.

By the time Sonalal finished, his voice was hoarse. But he still wanted to mention something else. So far, none of the journalists had commented on the only good thing that had happened last night, the beautiful music he'd played. Now he dropped a hint.

"Last night Raju danced incredibly," he said. "It was as if he was listening to music fit for the heavens."

None of the journalists picked up the hint. Sonalal wondered if any of the foreign journalists had told these Indian ones they'd witnessed music as dazzling as the rising sun. Long ago, he'd concluded most of the world was deaf to great music, but could it really be that deaf? Apparently so.

Now that Sonalal realized nobody cared to discuss his music, it dawned upon him that these people viewed him as some kind of freak—an interesting diversion from the same old world they chronicled day after day. His grief and guilt returned, and with it an overwhelming feeling of devastation. Suddenly he wanted all these people out of his home. Now! Rudeness entered his voice, and a sneer developed on his face. He became telegraphic in his replies to the journalists' questions. Soon he was answering with single words or just a nod. The journalists started to leave.

By the time everyone was gone, he had made another six hundred rupees in tips. He'd accepted the money with such mixed feelings that he quickly relinquished the sum to Sarita.

"If they'd been foreign journalists," she said, "we would have made six thousand."

5

Wₜₕ ₐₗₗ the journalists at Sonalal's home, his neighbors soon realized they were living next to an illustrious man. Later that morning, as Sonalal walked down the street to the *paan* stall at the local market, the people he bumped into accorded him the kind of respect normally reserved for men of means. For over two years, he'd lived in this neighborhood of small shopkeepers and low-level government workers, but until now, most people had treated him as if he were a sweeper who'd set foot in a Brahmin temple.

By the time he got to the market, Sonalal was feeling like the national sensation he truly was. The *paan* stall stood at the far end of the market, next to a sweetshop that displayed colored sweetmeats laced with thin silver foil in its window. The *paanwala,* an educated man who couldn't find a job doing what he'd been educated in, seemed pleased to see Sonalal, one of his more regular customers. The *paanwala* produced more than half a dozen newspaper articles he had clipped out.

Sonalal didn't hesitate to impose. "Could you read them to me?"

The *paanwala* obliged. He even translated articles from a couple of English dailies. Over and over, while Sonalal chewed *paans* and puffed *beedis,* he heard accounts of how Raju had bitten him—and how he'd bitten Raju back. The facts became more painful with every new rendition. Only now did Sonalal grasp the true magnitude of his sin—and the irreversibility of Raju's death. He began to sweat. For fifteen years, he had spent virtually every day with Raju, and now he couldn't conceive of a future without his beloved snake. What would he do with the rest of his life?

The *paanwala* kept reading. Three *paans* and two *beedis* later, Sonalal could listen no more, even though there were still a couple of articles left. He snatched the clippings and waved them angrily in the *paanwala's* face.

"You've already read them, right?"

"Yes," said the *paanwala*.

"All of them?"

"Yes."

"Then tell me something."

Sonalal was now sweating profusely. As he wiped his forehead, he said, "Again and again, it's the same sickening story! Do they all just go on about a madman who bit his snake? Nothing else?"

"What do you mean?"

"Last night, I played my *been* so beautifully the heavens wept from joy. That's important news, don't you think?"

"Sure."

"So did anyone report that?"

The *paanwala* scratched his chin thoughtfully. This gave Sonalal hope there really had been reports of tears from heaven, which seemed of some, albeit very minor, consolation. But all the *paanwala* said was "Hmm."

"Well, did anyone write that? Even one line?"

At last the *paanwala* said, "It finally rained in Bhopal yesterday. Do you think that counts?"

Although they usually ate at school, both Ramesh and Neel came home during lunchtime to find out if there were any new developments in the life of their famous father.

"Papa," said Ramesh, "my friends think the government should have entered you in the Games because you are the bravest man in all India!"

Though Sonalal didn't feel brave in the least, his sons' admiration was a novel experience for him, so he didn't argue. The boys had always been partial to Sarita, and she had much to do with how they viewed him. At school, the boys were embarrassed to mention their father's occupation in front of their classmates. For a while, the school principal had even been under the impression that he was employed in a government tourist agency. Sonalal didn't know if his sons were behind the lie—Sarita seemed at least as likely a culprit—but now he was glad his sons could be honest and proud of their father at the same time.

"They say what you did was as important as a man walking on the moon!" said Neel.

Ramesh shook his head. "The Americans never went to the moon."

And so began the boys' favorite argument.

"They went to the moon!" insisted Neel. "I saw the photos!"

"The Americans faked it," said Ramesh. "I saw those photos too.

A couple of men in white suits and motorcycle helmets walking in the desert—that's all. It could have been Rajasthan, if you ask me."

Neel turned to Sonalal. "Papa, what do you think?"

Even though it was the first time his sons had asked him to settle that kind of argument, Sonalal didn't relish the honor. Each day the boys learned more in school, and each day he worried more about looking foolish before them. As it was, he couldn't even sign his name, and Sarita, who could, made much of his illiteracy, often in front of the boys.

"The moon is a very far-off place," he finally said. "Between here and there, anything is possible."

Both Ramesh and Neel seemed satisfied with the reply.

While Sonalal and the boys ate their lunch of *aloo-mattar* and rice, they chatted pleasantly about nothing in particular. Soon all three were snickering like mischievous school chums. Sonalal felt closer to his sons than ever before. Until then, he hadn't realized how much he'd missed them.

At quarter to two, Ramesh said, "Papa, it's time for us to get back."

"Today you two can skip the rest of your classes," said Sonalal.

The boys grinned affectionately at their father, and the threesome became closer still. They played rummy most of the afternoon.

———————————————

Around four, a man from the circus showed up. He introduced himself as Mr. Fernandez and said he was the circus master. He was short and round, with widely spaced eyes and slanted eyebrows, absolutely sure of himself.

"I have a proposition," he said. "Are you interested?"

"I'm not sure," replied Sonalal.

"What I mean is, would you consider charming in the big tent? You'll be our highest-paid act: I'm willing to pay fifty rupees a performance."

A smile crept across Sonalal's face. Of course, he'd consider it! Here, after all these years, was what he wanted—an opportunity to play his music before a crowd that had specifically come to see him, not the tomb of a long-dead emperor.

"And in the middle of the performance," added the circus master, "you'll bite the snake."

Sonalal cringed as yesterday's events replayed in his mind's eye, filling him with horror all over again. His saliva suddenly tasted bitter. His stomach churned, and he felt his lunch rise to his throat. He sent it back down with a loud burp. Finally, still unsure whether he could manage to avoid throwing up all over the circus master—but also thinking the cocky bastard deserved it—Sonalal was able to reply.

"Never!" he cried, his voice cracking. "I'll never do anything like that again! I'm the best charmer in the world. Isn't that enough?"

"No."

Sonalal's eyes bulged as he shouted, "What is wrong with you people? I bit myself in half last night! Myself!" He ripped his *kurta* off, baring his slender chest. "Maybe you can't see the wound, but I feel it more with every passing minute. I'm bleeding all over this room. And you find it amusing! What kind of person laughs at a man who has lost his son? When you get home today, look in the mirror and ask yourself that question!"

The circus master appeared slightly bewildered by Sonalal's outburst. But then his expression became thoughtful, his lips moving silently as though he were performing some complicated calculation in his head. "I'm a flexible man," he finally said. "It doesn't have to be a snake. Maybe it could be some other animal—say, a tiger. We need a new tiger act. Unfortunately, we lost our trainer last week in an unusual accident. A thing like that won't happen again in a thousand years. Our tiger is old and very tame, harmless really."

At first, Sonalal thought the circus master was joking, but his face remained utterly serious. Sonalal couldn't believe it: The world had gone mad! Did this man really expect him to bite a tiger?

As if reading his thoughts, the circus master said, "Don't worry, you won't bite the tiger. We only have one, and tigers are very hard to come by these days. We'll just *pretend* that you'll bite it. The whole world already knows you've done something crazy like that once, so they'll come to see if you'll do it again. Nothing attracts people like the possibility of an innocent death. That's why Hindu-Muslim riots have stayed popular all these years. But you'll have to act like you might attack the tiger. The whole thing will depend upon how much tension you create. You obviously have a flair for the dramatic, so I doubt that will be a problem. But just to make sure, show me how ferocious you can look."

Sonalal actually did look quite ferocious as he replied, "The only animal I might bite is you!"

"Good! Good! A sense of humor. That's important in a performer. Now, growl—loud—like a man-eating tiger."

"Get out!"

The circus master took two steps back and reached for the door. But then he turned to Sonalal and said, "Seventy-five rupees a show. Seventy-five!"

"Out!"

"Don't be afraid to change your mind," the circus master said as he left. "It's a lot of money."

Sarita had been there all along, heard everything, said nothing. After the circus master left, she continued her silence.

"Can you believe that?" said Sonalal, still angry. "That rascal wants to entertain people not with my music but with my misery! What kind of world is this that values bloodshed more than beauty?"

Sarita knit her brow and pursed her lips.

"Say something, Sarita!"

"Think twice, Sonalal," she finally said. "No, think three times. Journalists won't shower you with thousands of rupees every day. Seventy-five rupees a performance—where else can we get that kind of money? In a year, we could live like *sarkari* officers! You should go back to that fellow and tell him you'll take his offer. What's the problem anyway? You just have to act a little. So act! For once in your life, do something for all of us. Your family! Forget your pride—"

"Never!"

She stared up at the ceiling.

"Please understand, Sarita. It's not just pride. How could I even pretend to do such a thing after what happened last night? It would be a mockery of everything Raju meant to me. Oh, my poor, poor Raju . . ."

With great effort, he managed to keep his composure. But Sarita seemed untouched by his emotion. So he ventured a different argument.

"Sarita, that man wants to put me in a cage with a tiger. A tiger! Haven't you considered that? I could die!"

Her face remained expressionless.

"I could die!" he roared.

"Nobly."

6

---

*H*IS POCKETS filled with some of the money he'd given Sarita last night, Sonalal left the house with no other intention than to take his time getting home again. But even after walking half a mile in the direction of the bus stop, he was still smarting from Sarita's words. Whenever he let his guard down, and it wasn't often, she managed to lash him with her vicious tongue—one, two, three!—just like that. And now, after all that had happened, she was trying to make him even more miserable. A man can bring home thousands of rupees and turn the world upside down, and still some women refuse to be pleased. There was nothing he could do for this woman—nothing at all. To hell with her!

But though he'd banished her to hell, something he did nearly every day, he couldn't rid himself of the echoes of her harsh words, her mocking tone.

There had been better times—long ago—when marital bliss wasn't an impossibility. For most of their life together, they had been united by the daily struggle for food and clean water. And after so many years of trying, they'd finally gotten further than they ever hoped. Life was still hard, very hard, but the boys would never go hungry as he once had. Yet something important had slipped away. These days, he and Sarita couldn't even talk about the coming of the Monsoon without each searching the other's words for hidden meanings. Sometimes there was more poison between them than in a whole nest of vipers. He knew Sarita believed he was to blame for their marital discord. Only he. She saw herself as shouldering all the burdens of the family, him as just a figurehead. Often enough, she was right. But he also knew it wasn't so simple. In marriage, there are many kinds of offenses, some not so easy to pinpoint. Because he was that sort of man, his sins had been the obvious ones. But there had been other sins, not his. It hadn't been his goal in life to turn into a womanizing drunkard, or at least he didn't think so.

He fumed the rest of the way to the bus stop and also while he rode the bus, paying no attention to the familiar city landmarks passing by. On Janpath Road, the bus became ensnared in traffic. He didn't have the patience to wait. So he hopped off in the middle of the intersection and dodged honking vehicles as he made his way to the curb, cursing Sarita with every step.

When he got to the curb, he faced the huge Janpath bazaar. Now a man with money to spare, he saw the material world before him in a new light. For the first time in his life, he could shop here.

Sonalal passed many clothing stores, gawking at the different styles of shirts and pants displayed in storefronts. At one store, a blue-and-white-checkered shirt caught his fancy. He went in. He liked the shirt even more when the shopkeeper let him run his fingers over the material.

"Pure cotton," said the shopkeeper. "It's back in fashion."

Sonalal took out a wad of money.

"Do you have trousers to go with such a nice shirt?" asked the shopkeeper.

Sonalal glanced down at his old *dhoti,* then shook his head.

The shopkeeper produced a pair of dark blue pants. "These match perfectly."

Sonalal went behind a sheet hanging in the rear of the store to try on the clothes. It was the first time he'd dressed so stylishly, and when he examined himself in front of a mirror, he liked what he saw.

"You're a man to reckon with," said the shopkeeper.

"I wasn't yesterday," said Sonalal, "but everything is different today."

"That's how life is," said the shopkeeper. "It changes just like that."

Sonalal paid for the clothes and stepped back into the street. But soon he became self-conscious. He felt like a middle-aged charmer from the village dressed up like a college student. So he lit a *beedi,* then leaned against a brick wall plastered with film posters and decorated with orange *paan* juice stains. He took slow deep drags, inhaling *beedi* smoke mingled with the exhaust of cars, buses, autorikshaws, and four-seaters. Each puff of the *beedi* soothed, gave him a bit more confidence. While he smoked, he carefully observed the mannerisms of well-dressed people, especially the way they walked. After half an hour, he once again felt less like himself, more like them.

And so, emboldened by the arrival of dusk, Sonalal began strutting along Janpath Road with the idealized gait of the well-to-do. He had a performing artist's gift for mime and in no time mastered the step. Half a dozen peddlers, some just boys, chased after him, fighting for his attention, undercutting each other's prices. At first, he was flattered. Then his conscience began to prick him. After all, these were his kind of people. So he told them, with rustic inflections that could leave no doubt, "You're wasting your time. I'm not one of them."

"Who are you then?" asked one of the peddlers.

Sonalal didn't know quite how to reply.

The heavy smog over the city added magnificent colors to the dusk sky, arousing all sorts of longings in him. Soon this translated into a yearning for lower spirits. But today he didn't feel like going to his usual haunts. He was again thinking about that special liquor—the golden elixir for which he'd charmed that last bus of journalists yesterday, the performance that changed his life. He walked past three- and four-star hotels until he garnered enough nerve to enter one of them for a drink. He was surprised the doorman didn't stop him, even more surprised when the hostess at the restaurant chaperoned him to a choice table as if he were an *Angrez*. Although the waiter seemed to have a doubt or two, his raised eyebrows quickly lowered when Sonalal flashed his money.

With all that money and no place to go, Sonalal knew he'd be there quite a while. First, he ordered that special liquor. When the much-longed-for drink arrived, he stared at it for several minutes, mesmerized by the unadulterated golden color of the liquid, the glistening ice cubes. It looked almost holy. But when he sipped the special liquor, its taste was not so special. He felt cheated. Worse, this drink, which in a way had started everything, reminded him of poor Raju. As he took another sip, he recalled how Raju used to curl up around his leg in the morning, and they would quietly enjoy each other's warmth before they got ready to go to the tomb. His eyes filled with tears. Suddenly Sonalal felt absolutely alone in life—utterly miserable.

So now he needed more liquor. He noticed the foreign women at other tables seemed fond of colored drinks.

"What are they?" Sonalal asked the waiter.

"Daiquiris."

Sonalal didn't think he could accurately pronounce the word, so he simply said, "I'll have a red one and a mango-colored one."

In a short time, he was pleasantly dizzy. He had more. The alcohol glued together pieces of his existence. For a moment, life mattered again. But the lightness of his intoxication gradually turned heavy. His life became broken once more, and now the pieces were sharper.

In this mood, he didn't think of seeking out his usual drinking friends, and certainly not Sarita. He thought of Reena, a prostitute in Old Delhi who knew exactly how to make him the happiest man in the world.

He'd been going to Reena for eleven years. Before he and the family moved out of the trans-Jamuna slums, the brothel in Chandni Chowk had been quite convenient. Even when he was having trouble making ends meet, he managed to visit Reena once or twice a week. Back then, she gave him special rates. And when he was broke, he even took him "on credit," though she never asked him to pay up later.

Sometimes he wondered why Reena was so fond of him. She must have known hundreds of men. Rich men, handsome men, important men. Who was he? Well, maybe *now* he was somebody—even if he wasn't proud of it. And he certainly wasn't anything to look at: short, arms and legs with no meat, a face like a muddy cricket bat. When he went to see a film, he was probably the only man in the whole cinema hall unable to imagine himself as the hero. No, there wasn't any good reason for Reena to care about him. Well, maybe his fingers. Women liked his long fingers, the way he used them. Of course, it had to be more than just this. He wished he knew what—why. One day, at the right time, he'd ask Reena.

As attached to her as he was, of late he hadn't seen all that much of Reena. Moving to the other side of Delhi two years ago had made things inconvenient. Getting to Chandni Chowk wasn't that much of a problem, but finding transportation back home in the middle of the night was, and the trip could be dangerous. That meant staying the night, which created its own difficulties for a married man. Often, he went months without seeing Reena. She was at the opposite end of the city, but it might as well have been Madras. Yet so committed was he to Reena that, just after moving, he'd had sex exclusively, though infrequently, with Sarita, rather than seek out other women. The effect of this was to make him miss Reena even more. After several months of only Sarita, he was desperate. If he was going to remain with his wife, he had to find someone else. Which led him to investigate brothels closer to home.

He embarked on a quest for another Reena with the determination of a marathoner intent on a new world record. So diligent was he— almost monastic in his pursuit—that, at first, he found little satisfaction in the huge variety of his sexual experience. But in time, he was able to enjoy again, and enjoy he did. Still, there was no one like Reena, no one even close.

———————

Sonalal dissolved into the chaos of Chandni Chowk. He was still tipsy; his legs felt light, his feet seeming to glide along the narrow medieval streets. He peered deep into the darkness of remote alleys, sensing centuries of culture and scars. Everything on the other side of the city suddenly seemed false. He stopped and stared down one particularly inviting lane for a long while, tempted to enter. How easy it would be to take a few turns and discover a new life!

At last he came to the brothel. Whenever he went there, he glanced up at Reena's second-floor balcony, where her petticoats usually hung over the railing to dry. At night, this was one of the more brightly lit streets around Chandni Chowk, and he was able to make out the petticoat colors. It was easier to tell how Reena really felt from the color of those petticoats than from being with her. Of course, sometimes the petticoats were taken in, and he wasn't sure how she was doing. Once, when there were no petticoats, he went in and spent a marvelous night with her. He came back the next day full of renewed desire and was startled to find that the petticoats hanging from Reena's balcony were all black and morbid brown. He lost his desire, just wanted to understand her own problems—for once give her some comfort. But then he thought she'd misinterpret his intent. So he went away.

Today he was glad to see mauve, pink, and turquoise petticoats. He marched right up to the old wooden door, which dated from before the Mutiny. Somewhere behind him, he heard stray mongrels barking at the planets.

He knocked hard. The Madam or any one of the other women might have answered, but it happened to be Reena. She wore a dark green sari with a silver border. Her hair was done up into a bun adorned with jasmine flowers.

She scrutinized his new clothes. "I like you better in a *kurta* and *dhoti*."

He stepped into the courtyard and said "*Namaste*" to two caged parrots named Raj and Nargis, after the film stars. Raj said "*Namaste*" back.

"Come," said Reena.

She went upstairs. He followed closely, his lustful gaze fixed on her wide round hips.

Her room was small but neat. The place always smelled of sandalwood and incense, though every time he stepped inside, the two odors mingled into a smell that tickled his senses in a novel way. And when Reena bolted the door, wonderful tingles spread through his loins, reminding him he still had the capacity to be young.

Reena faced him. "I've been waiting for you. I didn't think you'd take so long."

He was searching for a reply when she added, "I suppose famous people have no time."

"It's not like that, Reena. Besides, I don't deserve to be famous. It's just—"

"No matter. After tonight it will be decided."

"What? What will be decided, *jaaneman*?"

"Who is the world's greatest charmer."

Half the prostitutes he'd known had uttered something of that sort to him. But this was the first time Reena, who chose her words carefully, had said anything like that. Sonalal quickly unbuttoned his new pants. Within minutes, he was moaning from pleasure. After half an hour, he was on the verge of tears.

In the morning, he could barely walk. Sunlight gradually invaded the dark winding lane as he made his way to the main street. He turned a corner and stumbled over a mat on which cheap trinkets were laid out. The old woman who was selling them scowled and shouted, "Bastard!"

His throat felt parched. While he trudged along the street, the morning confusion of Chandni Chowk conspired with the blazing sun to bring on a headache. A loud screech came from somewhere nearby, hurting his brain even more. He felt overwhelmed by the shrill voices of peddlers who appeared to be hawking everything that ever existed.

Each person in the crowd seemed to be elbowing him, stepping on his toes, pushing him into the foul gutters that lined both sides of the street. He dodged bicycles, cows, rikshaws, horse-drawn *tongas,* a carter hauling huge kerosene tins. His head nearly got whacked by long alumium pipes a plumber was lugging somewhere.

Eventually he found his way out of the fracas. He stopped at a *paan* stall to smoke a *beedi,* recover himself. The *paanwala* was singing along with a Kishore Kumar song on the radio. It was a sad song, more than a decade old, from the film *Safar*. The *paanwala* seemed absorbed, lost in another world. Sonalal didn't disturb him; he liked the song too.

The song finished, and Sonalal got his *beedi*. As he stood there puffing away, he did his best to come up with a believable excuse for Sarita. After some thought, he decided there was no point and just concentrated on sculpting each mouthful of smoke he blew into the air.

He smoked another *beedi*. That only made him more thirsty.

"Give me an ice-cold cola," he said, eagerly anticipating the cold fizzy liquid coursing down his parched throat, what would have been only the fourth or fifth cola of his life.

"The ice man hasn't shown up yet," said the *paanwala*. "Everything is warm. A warm cola tastes worse than urine. Do you still want one?"

Sonalal passed. In any case, he was hungry as well, having eaten nothing in the past fourteen hours. Up the street, he spotted a cheap eating place, went there. The air inside was saturated with the smell of fried sweets and boiling milk. Sonalal's stomach growled. Still in a self-indulgent mood, he feasted on a plate of *samosas*, two glasses of mango juice, a sweet *lassi*, huge sticky *jalebis*, a *kulfi* with *phaluda* and red syrup. All that sugar did wonders for his headache. He finished with a cup of milky tea. Spirits lifted, he left for the Red Fort bus stop.

At the intersection before the bus stop, he came across a beggar woman from Bihar carrying a tiny baby with emaciated limbs and sunken eyes. The sight brought back memories of drought and famine. All of a sudden he felt terribly guilty over his easy money. He gave the woman twenty rupees and told her to take the baby to the government hospital right away.

"May you live forever," said the woman, showing off the money like a trophy.

News of his generosity spread quickly. In no time, he was surrounded by the maimed and wretched of Old Delhi. Before he knew it, he'd given away nearly two hundred rupees. He barely had enough left for the bus fare home.

The ride back home was bumpier than usual. The bus passed massive red government buildings built during the Raj, skyscraping hotels, modern shopping centers, countless cinema halls with garishly painted marquees. As the bus approached his stop, Sonalal began to worry about the inevitable encounter with Sarita. His feelings for Reena were so strong, he considered just telling the truth.

The bumpy ride had unsettled the ambrosia in his stomach. When he stepped off the bus, his belly felt bloated and was emitting all kinds of gurgling sounds. By the time he set foot in his home, he was uncontrollably flatulent.

"Where were you all night?" Sarita shouted. She grabbed the lapel of his new shirt. "And why are you dressed like a clown?"

Sonalal didn't break into an icy sweat as he usually did after a night away. "I know what you're thinking," he said casually.

"It will be the first time."

"If you want to believe I got drunk and went to a brothel, I can't stop you."

"So that's what happened!"

"That's what happened," he said in a monotone.

She gazed at him hard with her mind-reading eyes. He in turn did his best to cultivate a devious look. She examined his face for a full minute. Her expression became uncharacteristically puzzled.

"What are you keeping from me, Sona? What did you really do last night?"

"Just what I told you."

She waved her arms wildly. "Don't play games with me, you swine! I'll find out. Right now, I have to get away from here, from this horrible stink you're making!"

It wasn't the only time he'd outsmarted his wife, but it had never felt better. He went to the bathroom, where he made long sinuous noises that had a certain musical quality. Then he took a long nap, his first in years.

He was surprised Sarita didn't interrogate him further. It was unlike her to give up so easily; he wondered if their unexpected prosperity had softened her. Or perhaps she now thought anything was possible, that one stroke of luck would somehow lead to another, and another, and maybe at the end of it all, they might discover a little happiness.

Indeed, over the next few days Sarita became gentler, more attentive, maybe even forgiving. Sonalal saw the woman he'd married through new eyes. Suddenly Sarita and he seemed on the verge of tenderness, affection. When he cried one night over Raju's death, she held his hand for nearly an hour until he finally stopped sobbing. Once or twice, her old pet name for him even slipped out: Malai. As best he could recall, she hadn't used it since they'd left the village. *Malai,* "cream"; it sounded a bit ridiculous after all these years.

He continued to rise in his sons' estimation. Ramesh and Neel were still their mother's boys, but their loyalty wasn't as unequal as before. They seemed genuinely happy he was spending more time at home, and, for the first time, they were eager to introduce him to their friends. Sonalal spent a lot of time talking with his sons—learning about cricket stars, telling them about life in the village and the pleasures of charming.

"I'm the seventh generation of charmers in our family," he said, admiring the boys' long slender fingers, double-jointed like his own. "Maybe one of you will be the eighth."

Both boys smiled, giving Sonalal a glimmer of hope.

Around the neighborhood, his status was still soaring. He was a man to notice, and people did. During the morning walks he'd begun to take regularly, he swung his arms the way retired army officers do, his head tilted slightly upward, his chest expanded, his stride long, quick, and sure. People greeted him courteously, deferentially, as if he were a man of breeding. And he nodded back the way an important man does.

Even so, it was a double life of sorts. Although in front of people he appeared proud and confident, in private he continued to anguish over his sinful hypocrisy. Yet while his soul remained tormented, his body seemed thrilled with all the changes in his external life. When he was a young man, his moustache had given hints of turning up, and at various points in his life, he'd been all but certain the hair of his moustache had finally decided to mount his cheeks. But it never had. If anything, in recent years it had taken a downward turn. Yet now his moustache was unambiguously climbing upward—racing!

"It's very strange," said Sarita, "how your moustache is trying to connect with your eyebrows. Every day it gets closer and closer. I've never seen such a thing."

He shaved the moustache off the next morning. But the effect was cosmetic, for his moustache wasn't the only part of him upwardly inclined. It wasn't easy to keep his mind off Reena, though he did his best.

7

THE EXHAUSTION of grief had allowed Sonalal, an insomniac ever
since he could remember, to sleep soundly for a whole week
after Raju's death. But one night, he had a vivid nightmare. About
snakes. They were writhing and dancing, attacking him in forbidden
places. At three A.M., he sat up in bed, distressed. What did it all
mean?

He paced around for two and a half hours before finally managing
to fall back into a restless sleep.

"What is bothering you?" Sarita asked when she brought him
morning tea in bed.

"A bad dream," he replied in a tone meant to convey that he
wasn't interested in discussing it.

"Is everything all right?"

"Yes!"

"Sona?"

"What!"

"I had a dream too. A good one. Can I tell you about it?"

He shrugged.

She lay down next to him and coyly said, "I dreamed you were a
prince with a marvelous voice. We lived in a *mahal* on a mountain in

Kashmir. You sang to me, and I to you, just like in films. We were so deeply in love. And do you know what?"

He shook his head.

"Sona, we had our own three-wheeler! Our sons were *nawabs*, each with a servant." She smiled. In a soft sweet voice, she added, "You came back one night from charming with a gold necklace."

He took the hint. That afternoon, he visited jewelry stores in Dariba Kalan, where gem-studded pieces had once been fashioned for Moghul emperors. In the back room of one store, he saw artisans with glass eyepieces engraving golden ornaments.

"Nothing too elaborate," he told the jeweler. "Just a gold chain— maybe with a small gem."

The jeweler, a corpulent man with jowls like chicken thighs, set a box of gold chains before him. "How much do you want to spend?"

Sonalal had planned on spending at most five hundred, but suddenly he felt generous. "Not more than eight hundred."

The jeweler sifted through the box and laid a very thin chain before Sonalal. "For two thousand, you can have this."

"Two thousand? That chain is almost invisible!"

"Visible costs more."

Sonalal eyed the jeweler suspiciously but said nothing.

"Listen, my friend," said the jeweler. "I have no control over the price of gold. Maybe American cows do."

"American cows?"

"They call it economics," answered the jeweler.

"What?"

"E-co-nom-ics. It's like this. The price of milk is rising fast in America. And when prices in America go up, all the Japanese want gold. So the price of gold shoots up in India, which makes you un-happy. If American cows start producing more milk, maybe you'll get this chain for sixteen hundred."

Sonalal asked the jeweler to explain again. Business was slow, and the jeweler didn't seem to mind.

In the end, Sonalal came home with a silver necklace that con-tained 70 percent nickel. But it had a substantial feel and nice shine. He knew it would lose its luster soon, though probably no sooner than he lost his.

When he handed Sarita the box containing the necklace, she quickly peeked inside, then let out a girlish squeal. He hadn't pre-sented her anything in years. And while this was by far the most expensive gift he'd ever given her, Sarita's delight was so great that at first he felt only pity.

After dinner, Sarita shuttled the children off to bed. Then she coaxed him into the bedroom, where incense burned and flower petals lay on the cot. She removed her sari and petticoat in dim light while he admired her huge buttocks, her droopy breasts. They embraced. He tasted the fennel in her mouth, caressed her ample flesh. She caressed him back with skill that surprised him.

But he could not be suitably aroused. For he imagined her hands to be snakes—so troubled was he by the previous night's dream. After twenty minutes, she gave up. He readied for an assault on his man-hood, possibly a hundred other fronts as well.

"Sona, you are impotent," she said after a ponderous silence.

But she said it so calmly he was taken aback. In the scant light, he did his best to evaluate her expression. She appeared genuinely pleased.

She kissed him tenderly, then fell asleep.

All night Sonalal feared permanent impotence. He valued his virility even more than most men. Without it, he was little more than a pathetic drunk, a worthless husband, an absent father. A murderer on the loose! He couldn't go on unless his manhood was restored. And there was only one person who might be able to prevent his imminent suicide. So, well before the sun came up, he rushed off to see Reena at the brothel in Old Delhi.

While he hurried through the streets around Chandni Chowk, he was struck by how empty they were at this time of day. Most of the footpath dwellers had risen and gone their various ways, so the streets seemed unusually wide. And quiet. But even as he walked, he heard hawkers beginning to shout out the prices of their fruits and vegetables. In less than an hour, the streets would fill up, and everyone would be pressing against everyone else, bathing in communal sweat.

Soon he arrived at the brothel. The Madam opened the door. Without all her makeup, she looked much older.

"I have to speak to Reena," said Sonalal.

The Madam gave him a sharp look. "Speak? Hah! You men get the slightest itch, and no matter what time it is, you must have it scratched. After more than thirty years in this business, I'm still hoping to find out there's something more to men."

"No, you don't understand! It's very important."

The Madam shook her head. "How could it be so important this time of day? It's not even six-thirty! Go smoke a *beedi* and relax. Then come back in the evening—or at least in the afternoon."

"I must see Reena now!"

"If you weren't a regular, I'd . . . All right, all right, no need to turn this into India-Pakistan. Let me see what can be done. Wait."

Fifteen, maybe twenty minutes passed before Reena came downstairs, clothes wrinkled, hair uncombed. She didn't seem at all pleased to see him. He realized he'd forgotten to check what color petticoat was hanging from her balcony.

"What are you doing here so early in the morning?" said Reena.

"Can we go to your room?"

"No."

"Please, Reena."

She folded her arms, frowned. Finally, she said, "Stay here."

She went back up to her room. While he waited, a young man came down the stairs, his shirt unbuttoned, untucked. The man snarled at Sonalal before leaving. Sonalal burned. But when Reena showed up again, bathed, groomed, dressed in a yellow *salwar-kameez*—looking pure, almost edible—he felt less upset.

"All right," she said. "Come along, Sona. Let's find out what is so urgent. I wouldn't do what I just did for anyone else."

He wasn't exactly sure what she'd just done, but he could guess and didn't request details.

As soon as they stepped inside her room, Reena bolted the door and said, "Now tell me, Sona, what is the matter?"

"I've lost it!"

"Calm down, Sona. What have you lost?"

"It doesn't work anymore!"

"Of course it does." She undid his *dhoti* with a flick of her fingers and got down on her knees. "Here, I'll show you."

And so, Reena once again treated him to the secrets of Moghul courtesans that had been passed down through the centuries. His response, albeit sluggish, looked—and felt—promising. He was all but certain incontrovertible evidence of his manhood would soon appear. And yet, the much-longed-for event did not occur. Reena persisted with renewed energy and artistry. But the battle was already lost. An hour after they started, he had shrunk down to an embarrassment. The expression on his face told everything.

"I'm sorry," said Reena, panting from exhaustion. "But we were very close—very close. Sometimes this happens."

"It has never happened *to me* before."

"Don't worry, Sona. I think I know where we lost it. I understand exactly what I need to do next time."

It was good to hear about next time. He hugged Reena, supremely grateful for her effort, for her promise of future success. Yet at the same time, he felt undeserving of her goodness.

Later, while they lay in bed, he asked, "What is it you see in me?"

"That's a strange question."

"Is it my fingers?"

"No, Sona. Your fingers help, though. They are wonderful fingers. Marvelous fingers! Such fingers are not found in a million men—and I should know."

"Then what?"

"It's you."

"Me? I'm a married man growing old quickly. Scrawny; a flat, plain face; pockmarks everywhere. Most of the time I have no money. I can't read or write. I'm just a—"

"Sona, listen. I like lying down with you. After this business, I mean. Even now, when it didn't go as we had hoped. Sometimes I don't want to get up."

"That's it?"

"All this is silly. Who knows why anyone likes anyone? You just do or don't. I see the side of men they dare not show their families. As far as I can tell, it's their real side. It has nothing to do with money or caste or looks. Most men couldn't care less how they look to me. And most don't look good at all."

"And me?"

"You look good, Sona, very good. It's sad your family doesn't know how good you look."

He liked hearing that—though, sinner that he was, he knew he didn't deserve the praise. He kissed Reena gently on the forehead, then put his arm around her naked shoulders. He closed his eyes. But after a while, images from his nightmare began to invade his solitude. Soon none was left. All he could think of was snakes attacking his crotch, punishing his crime with perpetual impotence. His body tensed up.

"Tell me, Sona, what is really bothering you?"

He told her about his nightmare. He ended with "It's all so odd, no?"

"Odd? Why?"

"It must mean something."

She twirled the hairs on his chest with her fingers while she pondered the matter. The market was now open, and lively street noises rushed in through the window.

Finally she said, "Sona, I know how much Raju meant to you. After all that's happened, you aren't going to have an easy time living with yourself. That is why you're having such dreams. And besides, if you are a snake charmer, is it really so unusual to dream about snakes?"

8

A T HALF past nine, Sonalal approached the bus stop in front of the
Red Fort. The morning office rush was far from over, and the
lines were long. Now that even Reena had failed to restore his manhood, he was more disturbed than when he'd stepped off the bus just
a few hours ago. In his troubled state, he didn't have the patience to
wait so long for a bus. What was the hurry, anyway? He had nowhere
to go.

For half an hour, he roamed the grounds outside the fortress from
which Akbar the Great had once ruled all India. Finally he went inside.
He'd been in the Red Fort before, but today it seemed different.
Lonely. This early in the day, there were almost no visitors—just the
usual hawkers, amateur guides, and street performers waiting for someone to pounce upon. He thought they cheapened the place, and this
bothered him. For they seemed no different from those who waited
for tourists at Humayun's Tomb—no different from him.

Someone tapped his back. He turned around. It was another
charmer.

"Pardon me," said the man. "Aren't you the famous Sonalal of
Humayun's Tomb?"

"No."

"You look just—"

"Never heard of him."

The charmer gave Sonalal a strange look.

Sonalal walked away, once again concerned about the fate of his manhood. And why couldn't he get last night's dream out of his head? What did it all mean? If even Reena couldn't alleviate his anguish, he needed a different kind of professional help. He thought and thought. Whom to turn to? At last he decided to seek the opinion of Doctor Seth, a controversial sex therapist known all over Old Delhi.

So Sonalal went back through the side streets of Chandni Chowk, zigzagging deep into the oldest part of the medieval city. Somewhere in that maze was Doctor Seth's office, but he didn't know exactly where and was too embarrassed to ask. Eventually he had to. He scanned local faces. He spotted a wrinkly old man crouched in a doorway. The old man had the look of one who sees beyond the vagaries of life.

"Go up the street and turn right at the second lane," said the old man in a pleasant voice. "It's the house on the left with a blue door."

Sonalal was profuse in his thanks.

As he rushed off in the direction of Doctor Seth's office, the old man shouted in a voice so loud the whole neighborhood must have heard, "Pervert!"

A young man answered the door. He looked like a servant but claimed to be Doctor Seth's assistant. A crackling Saigal record was playing on an ancient gramophone at the back of the drawing room.

The assistant turned off the gramophone, then led Sonalal into the doctor's office, a windowless cubicle with peeling green paint and spider webs in all four upper corners. A naked light bulb flickered in the middle of the ceiling. From wall to wall stretched a tall wooden bookcase crammed with thick volumes that looked like they hadn't been touched in years. The signboard on the doctor's desk said, CONSULTATION FEE OF THIRTY RUPEES MUST BE PAID IN FULL AT END OF VISIT.

"Wait," said the assistant.

Sonalal sat down on a hard, straight-backed chair. While he waited, he began to have second thoughts. What was he doing here—in the office of this kind of doctor?

Sonalal's doubts only increased with the appearance of Doctor Seth, an old walking stick of a man with hair the color of tin. He wore rose-tinted lenses set in a cracked plastic frame. The tint couldn't hide a certain fiendish gleam in his eyes, unbecoming to a man of healing.

"Maybe this isn't a good idea," said Sonalal, standing up to leave.

"Nonsense," said Doctor Seth in a cranky voice. "Sit down!"

Sonalal sat.

"I am not just any doctor. I may be known as a sex therapist, but I am really a scientist. Do you know what science is?"

Sonalal had never heard the word but couldn't bring himself to admit it.

"Science," the doctor said, pointing to the bookcase, "is the greatest accomplishment of man. Science tells us the universe began with a Big Bang and will end in a Big Crunch. Science tells us why there are thousands of different kinds of beetles and why the stars shine. Did you know that our bones were made in the fiery centers of stars? Yes! Strange as it may sound, it's true. Science has proven it.

And I'll tell you something even more amazing. Science has shown that if you move very fast, time goes backward. Imagine that! I could tell you much much more, but already you can see that science is man's only glimpse into the Creator's mind. Do you understand?"

Sonalal understood even less now. What was this Big Crunch that would end the universe? It sounded at least as important as the general elections. So why hadn't he heard of it before? And how could his bones have come from stars? It made no sense at all. But that thing Doctor Seth said about making time go backward sounded very intriguing. If the doctor could perform such an amazing feat, then maybe he could bring Raju back! But was it really possible?

"How fast must one go to reverse time?" asked Sonalal.

"So fast your skin would burn up—faster than a ray of light goes."

Sonalal sighed. "No one can go that fast."

"Not yet. But one day it may be possible. Science advances quickly."

That gave Sonalal a little hope. If he could just go faster than a ray of light, he could be with Raju again. But then he envisioned a potential problem. "Suppose someone went backward in time," he said to Doctor Seth. "Would the future turn out different, or would it just happen all over again?"

"No one knows. It could even turn out worse."

"Oh no!"

Doctor Seth placed his hands on the desk and leaned forward. He spoke in a whisper. "You see, even we scientists must admit science isn't everything. The universe is mysterious, unpredictable. The mind of the Creator has endless depth that cannot be completely fathomed even by great scientists like Darwin, Freud, Einstein, and myself. And so you might find comfort in knowing that I apprenticed with disciples of the illustrious Madame Blavatsky. You have heard of her? Of course! Everyone has. So have no worries. The whole world is my laboratory. There is no one who knows science and philosophy like me, no one who can help you like I can. Now, explain please, what is the matter?"

Assured he was before a great healer—a man who might one day figure out how to use this thing called science to reverse time and bring Raju back—Sonalal decided to confide. "I had a dream."

"Yes? Yes?"

"About biting."

"In a land of parasites, such dreams are not uncommon."

"No, it was about snakes."

"Snakes, you say?"

Sonalal hesitated.

Doctor Seth pulled a handkerchief from his pocket and blew his nose three times. Then he took his eyeglasses off and started to clean the lenses with the mucus-filled handkerchief.

Sonalal stayed silent. Eyeglasses still in hand, Doctor Seth began to stare at him. Unshielded, the doctor's eyes were wild, mesmerizing.

"Go on!" said the doctor. "Fear not. Dreams are good. Great things have come from men who dream. Great things! Especially from men who dream about snakes biting."

"Really?"

Doctor Seth took a pen out of his pocket and drew a shape that looked like something between a circle and a hexagon. "This," he said, pointing to the circular shape, "is benzene. Or rather, what its chemical structure looks like. Have you heard of benzene?"

"No."

"Benzene is a very important chemical. It's what is called aromatic. That means it makes marvelous aromas."

Sonalal took this to mean that benzene gave mangoes, roses, and samosas their heavenly smells.

"One night," Doctor Seth went on, "a scientist named Kekule dreamed what benzene looks like. And do you know what he saw?"

Sonalal shook his head.

"A snake biting its own tail! And that, my friend, turned out to be one of the greatest discoveries of the last century. Isn't it incredible? But true it is, just as most incredible things are. Before Kekule, everyone thought the structure of benzene looked like a straight line, just as they once thought the world was flat. Thousands of scientists have since proven Kekule was right about benzene. And scientists have also shown that most other things are like a snake biting its own tail."

Sonalal was truly amazed this man Kekule had figured out why freshly sliced mangoes smell so wonderful simply by dreaming of a snake biting its tail.

"Maybe you too are a genius like Kekule," continued Doctor Seth, peering with his own hypnotic eyes into Sonalal's. "But this is neither here nor there. You have come to me for help. Go ahead, tell me everything. Absolutely everything."

Staggered by Doctor Seth's immense learning, excited by the possibility that he too might be a genius like Kekule, Sonalal began his story. "Perhaps you read about me in the newspaper—"

"I do not read newspapers. Why should I concern myself with the sneezes and burps of humanity when so many essential questions remain unanswered?"

So Sonalal began at the beginning. For over half an hour, Doctor Seth sat back in his chair and listened, brow furrowed.

Sonalal ended his story in a whisper. "I loved Raju *so* much."

"Men are meanest to those they love," said the doctor.

Doctor Seth's words sounded like a prison sentence to Sonalal.

When a long time passed without a reply, the doctor added, "I wonder if there isn't something else?"

Sonalal remained quiet.

"There is, isn't there?"

Sonalal nodded—just barely.

"Well?"

The doctor's intense gaze did not waver, and Sonalal could keep it inside no longer. "I've lost my manhood!" he cried out.

"Aha! . . . Hmm . . . very, very interesting. Now that really is like a snake biting its own tail, don't you think?"

Sonalal wasn't sure if the doctor was making fun of him. To make matters worse, the doctor offered no other comment. Sonalal started to fidget. What could the old man be thinking?

Doctor Seth finally spoke. "Do you enjoy moving your bowels?"

Sonalal was flabbergasted. Such an absurd question! Crude! And what business was it of the doctor's? What did his bowels have to do with anything?

As though he'd read Sonalal's mind, Doctor Seth said, "You must be frank. It is the only way I can help. According to Professor Freud, the father of the science of the mind, this question must be answered by all—especially if their sexual function is affected. And please remember, I am a doctor."

The doctor sounded serious and professional, so Sonalal cast his eyes downward and answered as best he could. "Moving bowels is just what one does. It is hard to get excited about something over which you have no choice."

He glanced at the doctor to divine his view on the matter.

But the doctor ventured no opinion. Instead, he said, "Do you prefer women with little breasts?"

That was too much for Sonalal. He slapped the desktop loudly and said, "No, I like breasts like grapefruits! Cantaloupes!"

"Hmm."

"What is the purpose of all this? Why do you keep asking me such strange questions?"

"Because you are a homosexual."

That was even worse than Sonalal feared. A series of complicated expressions passed over his face. His eyes narrowed; his nostrils flared; the corners of his mouth twitched. The doctor simply watched with a diabolic look that upset Sonalal even more. Sonalal was ready to scream the worst insults known to man. But he couldn't decide on the most appropriate one. His hands trembled. The right word just wouldn't come to him—yet another manifestation of his impotence! He thought of striking the sinister old man but feared he might break the doctor's frail bones and be sent to jail. Still, he couldn't just walk away, not after what Doctor Seth had said.

"There's nothing wrong with being a homosexual," added the doctor. "Many great artists have been. Da Vinci, Tchaikovsky, some of the most brilliant Romans and Greeks—Plato himself! You may not have heard of these people, but I assure you it's very elite company. And, of course, there's no reason why you can't love women along with men. In the West, that kind of thing is quite fashionable these days and also makes a certain metaphysical sense—"

Right then, Sonalal spit in the doctor's face and stomped out without paying the thirty-rupee fee.

For much of the afternoon, Sonalal roamed aimlessly around Connaught Circle, fretting over Doctor Seth's diagnosis. Back in his village, a homosexual would have been stoned. And now Doctor Seth said he was one! As he thought about it, though, he recalled boyhood experiences long suppressed. He wondered about grown men doing those things, imagined many other things grown men might do. Only then did he realize he stood at calamity's brink.

Clearly, someone like him could not be a family man. Now that he knew that, he felt wistful. For the few days it lasted, he'd genuinely enjoyed family life, the brief glimpses of its deep satisfactions. In a couple of months, he might have been able to undo Sarita's damage—gotten his sons back. Who knows? He and Sarita might even have found a way to let some sunlight back into their marriage.

Now it could never be. Even these past few days, the weight of domesticity had exacted a subtle toll upon him. A tiger kept in a cage too long becomes little more than a striped cat. But now he was free again. Free to breathe, free to live his own life, free to frequent old haunts.

He knew there was no point in going home in this frame of mind. He wouldn't be able to disguise his restless mood, and that would set Sarita off. So he trekked more than two kilometers to Humayun's

Tomb, where he was now better known than the dead emperor himself. It was the first time he'd been back since biting Raju.

"Sonalal's here!" several people shouted at once.

Within seconds, he was surrounded. At first, all the attention only intensified his sense of guilt. He deserved blows to the head, not affectionate slaps on the back! But the commotion managed to drown out the protests of his guilty conscience. And all the admiring eyes around him seemed to compensate in part for his lost manhood.

Everyone was trying to touch him, as if he were a holy man with the power to bestow eternal bliss. Tourists figured out who he was and begged for his autograph. Since he couldn't write his name, he signed with an incomprehensible squiggle, the way film and cricket stars do.

His friends dragged him away from the growing crowd. The vendors among them invited him to eat at their stalls—free.

"Take a bite of my *samosas*," said Harish the *chaatwala*, not known to be a generous man.

"Taste some of my mangoes," said Deepak the fruit seller.

"It's a hot day—have an ice-cold cola," said Kamal the soft-drink vendor.

Others offered him peanuts, *pakoras*, roasted corn, tea, lots more. He couldn't refuse. He ate till he started to belch.

All of a sudden he had more friends than people he knew. And the friends he didn't know refused to let him go. One suggested renaming the place "Sonalal's Tomb."

For a moment, all were in agreement: From now on, Humayun's Tomb was to be known as Sonalal's Tomb.

But then someone said, "Sonalal isn't yet dead. How can he have a tomb?"

This was unanimously considered a major obstacle.

Mohan the souvenir seller, who often showed Sonalal picture postcards of the Taj Mahal and other famous places, had a different objection. "Sonalal is a Hindu and must be cremated, not buried, and therefore doesn't need a tomb."

Sonalal was about to suggest he could be cremated first and then his ashes could be buried, when Tariq the *paanwala* spoke.

"The government will take forever to change the name," said Tariq, "and then there might be Hindu-Muslim riots."

Sonalal didn't want to be responsible for all that. With more than a little regret, he put an end to the debate by announcing, "The tomb should remain Humayun's."

Everyone cheered Sonalal for his sacrifice.

Laloo the magician had been present throughout. But the usually talkative Laloo hadn't said anything. After the others finally left, Laloo came up and held out his hairy hand. Sonalal shook it.

"May your good fortune continue," said Laloo.

Sonalal knew Laloo had never liked him much, so he was all the more impressed that the cantankerous magician had it in him to offer congratulations which sounded so genuine.

"My fortune is not as good as everyone thinks," said Sonalal. "But it's kind of you to say that, Laloo."

A mocking smile appeared on Laloo's face. "Luck is a funny thing. It comes and goes just like that. Take the lottery. Luck can pick anyone, no matter how many tickets you buy, no matter how deserving you are."

"I am the best charmer in all India. My music can—"

"Hah!"

"You're jealous!"

"Of whom? Certainly not you, a mere charmer. And it's ridiculous to think snakes have any idea what you're playing. Snakes can't hear!"

Laloo broke into laughter.

Sonalal had heard this untruth before, and it always angered him. What did these people know? He couldn't vouch for other snakes, but of Raju he was certain. Raju had possessed the most discriminating ear he'd ever witnessed—in people or animals.

"What you say isn't true," said Sonalal, trying to remain calm.

"Of course it is," replied Laloo, still chuckling. "It has been proven by science."

Science. Again that wicked word! First, Doctor Seth's science had told him he'd been making love to the wrong sex all these years. And now, according to Laloo's science, he'd wasted his whole life playing beautiful music to deaf snakes!

"As surely as you and I are standing here," said Sonalal, "my cobra knew music. Raju detected the notes from my *been* even before I heard them. I don't understand why you're saying all this, Laloo. It must be envy."

Laloo spat on the ground. "What is there to be envious of? Were any of your ancestors the favorite *jadugars* of maharajas? Do you know the secrets of the stars and planets? Can you levitate or swallow fire? Have you seen the great white peacock with countless eyes who struts from cloud to cloud? At the cremation grounds, are you able to talk to people dead for many centuries? Can you access the highest spirits at will? Do they talk to you? Have you sniffed the ether that flows through the universe and connects everything? Can you . . ."

Sonalal was no longer paying attention. Laloo's questions once again reminded him how exquisitely he'd played the night Raju died. The world's fascination with bloodshed had confused him, confounded him, made him forget his real feat. Hadn't he sniffed the universal ether? Yes—yes! His music had brought tears of joy to the gods' eyes. He really was different from the hordes of other roadside performers: animal trainers with dancing bears, puppeteers who staged stories from the great epics, *fakirs* who walked on red hot coals, magicians like Laloo who joined the shredded pieces of a scarf after waving a feather wand.

Laloo was about to end his harangue. "Magic is God's greatest work," he said. "And that means magic is the most important work a man can do."

Sonalal didn't notice Laloo had finished.

"Well?" said Laloo in an irritated voice.

Sonalal smiled. "I'm grateful to you, Laloo *bhai*."

"Grateful?"

"Because you made me remember what everyone else almost made me forget: that the gods had given me an audience. Once—only for a moment—but it was the most marvelous experience of my life. Unfortunately, I paid a terrible price for that moment. If it were only possible, I would gladly give back that moment, wonderful as it was, to have Raju by my side again. But that moment is all I have now— that memory and nothing else. If you can speak to the gods whenever you wish, then you are right, there's no reason to be jealous of me. Please forgive me for suggesting otherwise."

Laloo was silent a while. Then he said, "Sona, *dost,* when they spoke to you, what did they say?"

"It is hard to explain."

"You must! Why are you hiding it from me?"

"I'm not hiding anything, Laloo *bhai.* You see, they didn't speak. They were just there—listening."

Later that afternoon, Sonalal found Jagat, an older charmer who for years had kept him company between buses.

Jagat himself was famous. A mediocre charmer and even worse snake catcher, he'd been bitten dozens of times while searching the jungle for snakes he later sold in the city. Jagat claimed he'd survived the bite of every kind of poisonous snake in India, which certainly explained all the scars on his body. A doctor from the government institute often came to draw Jagat's blood, which he said could cure patients dying from almost any snakebite. Once, Dr. Basu even sent Jagat's blood on a plane to Nepal, where a rich man's daughter was dying from the bite of a poisonous mountain snake. When the girl recovered, her father offered Jagat a large reward. Jagat refused, saying that was no way to earn money.

It had only been a week since Sonalal had last seen Jagat, but it seemed much longer. Had Doctor Seth not so recently pronounced him a homosexual, Sonalal would have hugged his dearest friend.

"Ah, the celebrity. At last you have a little time for us."

"Stop it, Jagat *bhai.* But it's all so strange, no?"

"It's too bad about Raju. He was a very fine snake."

"He was a *great* snake. He was like my son."

"Yes, I know. If you want to hear the truth, that is why I've kept away. I was angry over what you did."

"Jagat *bhai,* I miss Raju so, so much! I went mad for a moment and committed a terrible sin. But look how the world reacts! It rewards all the wrong things. And I'm so shameless I've gone along with it all."

"That is true."

Sonalal looked down at the ground. Jagat kept quiet, though his eyes remained reproachful.

Finally, Jagat said, "What's happened has happened. A moment of madness, as you say. When the whole world is mad, why shouldn't you be?"

"I'm madder than the maddest dog in Delhi."

"You don't have to convince me of that, Sona."

"What to do?"

Jagat seemed to be pondering something. After a while, he said, "What if Raju was one of those creatures who can never die? Some snakes are like that, you know." Jagat pointed to the sky. "Maybe Raju is up there now."

That was just what Sonalal needed to hear. "Do you really think so, Jagat *bhai?*"

"I wish I knew. All I can say is that in fifty years, I've only seen one snake good enough to dance for the gods, and that was Raju."

Yet the thought that Raju might be dancing to someone else's tune, even if it happened to be a god's, was more than Sonalal could bear. He bit his lower lip.

"At least Sarita must be proud to be married to a famous man," said Jagat.

Sonalal grimaced. "Is such a thing possible?"

"You may be right. Wives will never admit it. This is one of the few respects in which they are worse than husbands."

"Sarita doesn't mind the money, though. And my sons are happy. It's the first time they've been proud of me."

"That is something."

"I suppose, Jagat *bhai,* but . . ."

"But what?"

It took a long time for Sonalal's words to come out, and when they did, his voice was just a whisper. "Do you think I'm a homosexual?"

"What?"

Sonalal repeated the question, only a little more audibly.

Jagat raised his eyebrows. "You've been to Doctor Seth too, eh?"

"How do you know?"

Jagat's broad grin revealed most of his *paan*-juice-stained teeth. "Almost twenty years back, I went to Doctor Seth. Even then, he had quite a reputation. They say he can work miracles, but, frankly, I have doubts. Sometimes he sounds like a crackpot. He has told a lot of people they are homosexuals. Maybe he is one."

"Really?"

"You'd be surprised who is."

"Who?"

"Never mind. But if Doctor Seth is, he must be doing this to find men to love."

"He is *so* old."

"And you think old people don't like sex?"

"Not so much."

"I'm sure it must be very lonely being an old homosexual. It is very lonely being old. And here in India, it's not like America and England, where one can be a homosexual in the open and find other homosexuals easily. Here, they treat homosexuals worse than the lowest untouchables. But in America, it's different. They even have beach colonies where everyone goes about nude. America is very advanced."

Advanced was not exactly what Sonalal would have called it, but he felt he must defend India, especially since the Indian team was getting trounced during the second week of the Games. So he countered with the first thing that came to mind.

"It is very easy to get a prostitute in India."

"That is true," said Jagat. "And no one knows better than yourself."

9

SINCE REENA was so confident she could restore his manhood, Sonalal kept going back, hoping his potency would reappear as suddenly as it had disappeared. Even though he always left with his manhood still in doubt, he experienced no small pleasure from Reena's increasingly creative methods, which left him hungering for more.

Sarita was unable to hide her disappointment over the resurrection of his wanton ways. And yet, as if hoping it was only a temporary lapse, at first she kept quiet when he came home drunk or didn't come home at all. But within several days, a clear pattern was established, and after a week it had the reliability of a natural law: He spent every third night outside. No longer could Sarita look the other way. All her old rancor soon returned, and then some.

Of course, Sonalal was used to Sarita's bitterness. And strangely enough, now that it was back, he realized he'd been missing it. But over the next few days he began to contend with an altogether different kind of bitterness, not welcome in the least. Gradually, he'd become aware of an acidic taste in his mouth. It had grown as surreptitiously as a tumor, and before he knew it, his mouth flooded with a taste so bilious he feared Raju's snake juice had somehow damaged his tongue—or even his brain!

Each day, the taste became more bitter. Sonalal tried to counteract it by chewing sweet *paans* and sucking candy—to no avail. Worse, every night he dreamed he was attacked by a different snake. The snakes had already robbed him of his manhood; now what did they want? He found out soon enough. The many snakes metamorphosed into a single multihooded cobra with special markings on each hood. He knew the creature so well he could have drawn it perfectly. He even knew the cobra's name.

She was Rani, Raju's mate, bent on revenge.

Sonalal constantly feared Rani's attack. He sensed her presence everywhere. Breezes hissed. Footsteps slithered. Whenever Sarita swept the floor in the evening, the sound of the broom set Sonalal so on edge he'd go outside and smoke until she finished. He was afraid of falling asleep. He placed his cot on stacks of bricks, hoping Rani was too old to jump that high.

To his surprise, Sarita didn't say anything. That worried him too, for it meant she'd decided he was crazy. Or that she really could read his mind—that she understood. This latter possibility made him sometimes gaze upon the perspicacious woman in awe.

One day, Sonalal was absolutely certain Rani was stalking him throughout Delhi. Everything hissed and slithered, and he could almost feel her venomous fangs pierce his calf with each step. He finally fell asleep at three that night, only to dream once more of Rani, who hissed at him and said, "It's only a matter of time before you pay for your sins."

Most unnerving was that she spoke in Sarita's voice.

The next morning, he decided to go to the government institute and consult Dr. Basu, the same doctor who coveted Jagat's blood. Dr. Basu was known to charmers throughout Delhi as someone who really knew how to treat people bitten by snakes, and Sonalal wondered if the doctor also knew how to treat people who'd bitten snakes.

Dr. Basu was a squatty neckless man in his late forties. A waxy bald spot spread over much of his head. Sonalal had previously met him only briefly when he came to draw Jagat's blood at the tomb. But the doctor didn't seem to remember. Initially, he was very curt.

"We've met before," said Sonalal. "Doctor *sahib,* I am a friend of Jagat's."

The mention of Jagat made the busy man warm up. "If Jagat sent you, then I am at your service. Were there but ten Jagats, no one would ever die of snakebites in India. No one! Do you know how many cobras, vipers, kraits—even rattlesnakes from a place in America called Arizona—live in the snake pits behind this building? Hundreds! We extract their venom every day in hope of creating antivenoms and vaccines, but none has the power of Jagat's blood. Your friend is a human mongoose, famous in the medical journals—maybe the most famous charmer in the world."

That was a bit hard for Sonalal to take, especially since Dr. Basu didn't seem to know who he was.

"Jagat may be famous," said Sonalal, "but he is not a very good charmer."

The doctor frowned.

Sonalal felt ashamed. "Forgive me, Doctor *sahib*. I am unworthy of Jagat's friendship. I am unworthy altogether."

"What is this about?"

"You may have heard of me, Sonalal, the charmer who bit a cobra."

"Of course! Sonalal! Yes, yes, we met once—I just didn't recognize you. Even before all this newspaper bunk, other charmers told me of your great talent. One day I hope to hear your wonderful music."

Sonalal beamed.

"But Sonalal, why did you do such a foolish thing?"

Sonalal's face became hot. "Doctor *sahib*, all my life I have done foolish things. But this, my greatest sin, was done in the middle of a mad rage. My whole life has been ruined by a single moment of stupidity."

Dr. Basu took a long time to answer. "That's usually how lives get ruined," he finally said. "I'm very sorry for you, but how can I help?"

Sonalal told the doctor about his bitter taste, his impotence, his nightmares, his fear of Rani's lethal revenge. "I deserve it," he said, "but I'm still scared."

Dr. Basu nodded sympathetically.

Sonalal then went through the kind of probabilistic analysis he carried out nightly in his head. "You see, Doctor *sahib*, Rani would have to make it from the hills all the way to Delhi. Unless she somehow got a ride on a truck or a bus, it would be very hard for her to get here. It's a long way for a snake to crawl, and the roads are safe for no creature, particularly at night. And if you don't take the road, it's even more complicated. Steep hills to climb, streams to cross: Without a guide, you're more likely to end up in Cape Comorin or Darjeeling than Delhi. On the other hand, it's possible some charmer caught Rani and brought her to Delhi. But I know most local charmers and their snakes, and none looks like Rani. Besides, if she's still alive, she is very old. No charmer would want such an old snake. If Rani has been caught and brought to Delhi for charming, it would have been years ago. And then she surely would have found Raju on her own—long before I did what I did. So Rani must either be dead or still in the hills. If she's alive, with the distance and her age, it would be impossible for her to get here, don't you think?"

Like most doctors, Dr. Basu ignored the question that most concerned his patient. Instead, he guided Sonalal into an examining room. The room smelled of a minty disinfectant that temporarily diminished the bitterness in his mouth.

Before being examined, Sonalal had one more question. "Doctor *sahib*, do you think Rani might be able to forgive me if she knew how much I loved Raju? If only she had an idea how much I miss him— how much I wish I could have him back!"

Dr. Basu removed his eyeglasses and rubbed his eyes. "All of us wish we could change the past, but we can't."

"No, Doctor *sahib*. They say that time can go backward if you move so fast your skin burns off."

"I've never heard that," replied Dr. Basu, "but if it's true, then you'll just end up with no skin."

Sonalal hadn't considered that frightening possibility.

"Take off your clothes," said the doctor. "I'll be back in just a second."

When Dr. Basu returned more than an hour later, he checked Sonalal's pulse and blood pressure, peered into his throat with a penlight, listened to his heart with a stethoscope, poked his belly with cold fingers, banged his knees with a reflex hammer.

"What do you think, Doctor *sahib*?"

"I'm afraid I can't help you with your kind of problem."

"What's wrong? Is it very serious?"

"That depends on you."

"What's the matter with me, Doctor *sahib*? What?"

Dr. Basu looked Sonalal straight in the eye and said, "It's called guilt."

His guilt grew. Morning, afternoon, and night—day after horrible day—he dragged around its unearthly weight. The taste of guilt was always on his tongue, its smell constantly offending his nostrils. And now that a doctor had labeled it a disease, his guilt manifested a fever. Sonalal felt like a *puri* swelling in boiling oil. At night his pillow was saturated with sweat, and when he woke up, he was so thirsty he drank whole jugs of water. The fever jumbled his thoughts, and he wasn't sure of anything anymore—except that he was going to die. Even Sarita showed concern for his wretched state. "Sona," she urged, "you should see a doctor."

"Doctors don't know anything."

"That might be true," said Sarita. "But they still know more than you."

He couldn't deny her point. So, just two days after his first visit, he went back to Dr. Basu, more miserable than ever. The doctor examined him, drew blood for special tests, and told him, "Come back tomorrow."

When Sonalal returned the next day, still complaining of a fever and bitter taste, the doctor said, "I've thought a great deal about your case. I stand by my original diagnosis."

Sonalal had been doing some thinking of his own. "I find it strange that guilt can make me lose my manhood, fill my mouth with an awful taste, and cause me to shake and sweat with such a high fever."

Dr. Basu nodded knowingly. "I also thought it strange when I saw my first case of guilt after returning here from Europe." With both hands, he lifted a thick book off his desk. "Scientific textbooks say nothing about guilt causing such symptoms. But the books were written by doctors from abroad, and this is India. And there is no question the bodies of Indians work differently. In my medical experience, guilt can do all sorts of things. And yours is by far the worst case I've come across."

Sonalal remained unconvinced, especially now that Dr. Basu was sounding like nutty Doctor Seth, invoking science and whatnot. He needed a modern doctor unbiased by science. After making careful inquiries, he went to the office of a neurologist well known for treating the brains of politicians.

But when he asked for an appointment, the doctor's secretary said, "The doctor will only examine you after you get a special brain test—a kind of X ray."

Sonalal knew X rays were done for broken bones, and he couldn't understand why it was necessary to get one of his head. But who was he to argue with a renowned doctor?

"Fine," he said.

"It costs twelve hundred rupees."

Sonalal was desperate enough to spend that kind of money—a large fraction of what was left—if Sarita would relinquish the sum. Yet the need to clearly explain the matter to her prompted him to ask, "Why does it cost so much?"

"Because this special X ray is made by an expensive machine imported from Germany," replied the secretary. "The machine bombards your brain with the smallest things in the world. Everything shows up."

Sonalal didn't feel like having his brain bombarded by anything, no matter how small it was. "Let me think about it," he said, and left.

Disillusioned with people who called themselves doctors, over the next week he went to homeopaths, *veds,* fortune-tellers, palmists, *hakims,* astrologers, witches, senile old people who looked wise but knew almost nothing—just about everyone he could think of except that crank sex therapist, Doctor Seth. They all said the same thing.

Guilt.

10

THOSE LAST days before the Monsoon, the city was starving for water. People thought twice about flushing the toilet, thrice about watering their dry plants. The mornings were hot, the afternoons scalding, the evenings hot again. At night, bloodthirsty flying insects and carnivorous crawling bugs went on a rampage. Sarita slept through it all, possibly, Sonalal reflected, because the insects didn't care for her blood. But the bugs made sleep impossible for him. Often, he found himself listening to the strange noises of the night that punctuated the regular rhythms of Sarita's snores. Sometimes a particularly fascinating juxtaposition gave him an idea for a new melody. But that reminded him he might never play again, a thought which rapidly sent his mood into a downward spiral that made him want to scream.

Not far from his home was a huge banyan tree, a striking anomaly in the local landscape. Rather than cowering in a hostile world of cement and smog, the banyan thrived. But due to the perverse pains of growing up in the big city, the tree had become contorted. Its thick branches and overground roots meandered every which way, sometimes almost managing to connect, creating a massive wooden arabesque that seemed intent on forming its own jungle.

As in previous summers, on those hot sleepless nights, Sonalal often went outside to the banyan amid a cloud of mosquitoes that, sting by sting, depleted his feverish guilt-ridden blood. The venerable banyan reminded him of a similar tree near his ancestral village, and its many limbs seemed to offer support at a time when life itself had become too much. Under that tree, things made more sense than anywhere else.

Sonalal spent hours beneath its branches, examining his soul in the diffuse light of the gibbous moon while the night slowly ebbed. He was even sitting under the banyan when the Monsoon finally hit Delhi. He was almost certain the very first raindrops fell on the tree and took it as a sign the heavens approved of his introspection.

And so he sat, night after night, trying to comprehend the strange manifestations of his disease—his impotence, his bitter taste, his horrible nightmares, his fear of Rani's revenge—while gray Monsoon clouds settled over the capital. The deeper he delved, the greater his guilt seemed. There was no end to it. He was a murderer, an adulterer, a good-for-nothing father. What else? A coward. A demon! Could there be any redemption for such a man? In his next life, he'd be reborn as a cockroach—and probably just in time for Sarita to step on him in her old age.

And yet, sitting under the banyan all those nights—through the quiet of moist heat, the gentle patter of warm rain, the crash of the downpour—he found a kind of solace. But his glimpses of tranquility were brief. A guilt like his couldn't disappear just like that. Even so, to his surprise, the bitter taste gradually went away. So did the fevers. And that gave him hope that maybe he'd even recover his manhood with time. But he knew one thing would not go away—could not go away. If Rani was alive, he'd have to face her someday, and that day he would die. One can evade many things, but not kismet.

For a fortnight, New Delhi had functioned with European efficiency, but shortly after the Games ended, the city returned to normal. Power failures became routine again, as did endless traffic jams and milk shortages. Telephone lines were down for days at a time. The air suddenly got more polluted, and everyone was coughing. The real news that had been ignored furiously reasserted itself: half a dozen scandals in the prime minister's cabinet, a coal miners' strike in Bihar, religious riots in Andhra ending in indiscriminate police shooting, a feud between the governor and chief minister of Karnataka, hundreds killed in an earthquake in the Himalayan foothills, yet another dacoit queen terrorizing villages in Uttar Pradesh, an upcoming visit by the American secretary of state, new tensions along the borders with Pakistan and China.

The world forgot Sonalal. No more journalists, no more money. Neighbors ignored him when he passed them in the street. Some even snickered at the snake charmer who walked like a retired army officer. One morning, while standing at the *paan* stall puffing a *beedi,* Sonalal overheard two adolescent boys dressed in the same khaki uniforms Ramesh and Neel wore to school. He cocked his head back and listened.

"I don't think he bit a snake at all," said one of the boys. "I think he just cut a rope in half and made fools of those foreign journalists."

"That could be," said the other boy. "Foreigners will believe anything. They already think Indians levitate and sleep on beds of nails."

"What if he really did bite a snake?"

"Then I doubt there's a greater idiot in all India."

Both boys chuckled.

Disheartened at the fickleness of the world, Sonalal meditated long hours on the fleeting nature of fortune and fame. He'd always had a contemplative streak, and after his initial outrage, he found some comfort in an otherworldly view of things. It happened to be the month of shooting stars, and he too felt like a shooting star rapidly burning out. Rather, already burned out. And that, he realized, was the nature of the universe. Maybe this was what Doctor Seth meant by the Big Crunch: Everything must come to an end. After all, which film star has lasted more than a few years? All right, Amitabh, Dev Anand, Raj Kapoor, maybe one or two others. But there really weren't many. And what politician in recent years had remained on top long enough to do anything? Those days were gone. Sanjay Gandhi was the last of the great ones. And look how long he lasted. The very best a man could be was a shooting star. And yet the brighter a star burned, the faster it fizzled. A rule not just of life but the whole universe, and, who knows, maybe there was something right about that.

But these were weighty thoughts, and it didn't take long for them to weigh Sonalal down. Solitude turned into boredom and loneliness. He longed for Raju's company, and this only fed his guilt. And that reminded him he'd never deserved the attention in the first place, that only in a world as topsy-turvy as this was a man rewarded for hurting the innocent. He became more irritable, more depressed. Since he was home so much, he and Sarita inevitably quarreled.

"You've squandered all the money," she complained one day. "All we can afford to eat is *dal* and rice. Soon the boys won't even get a glass of milk in the morning. What good is it to be out of the slums if we live worse than when we were there? You need to earn all that money back."

Sonalal waved his finger at her. "*You* took most of the money for safekeeping!"

She ignored his point. "It was the children's inheritance, and now it's gone!"

He eyed her suspiciously. "But Sarita, you must still have thousands of rupees. I only took a little—"

"How do you think we've been living these past few weeks? Perhaps we can survive a bit longer on what is left, but after that, there's nothing. Nothing!"

"There was enough for a whole year!"

"If there was, *I* never saw it. What did you spend it on? I want to know."

She glared at him as though waiting for a formal accounting. He suspected she'd sequestered most of the money. Of course, he'd spent some, not that much really, but it was largely on things he couldn't tell her about.

"Your necklace," he finally said. "I spent a lot on your necklace."

"My necklace? That cheap trinket doesn't even shine anymore!"

"It wasn't cheap. American cows aren't eating grass like they used to, so the price of necklaces has become very high."

"What nonsense!"

"No, Sarita. It's true. When American cows don't make milk, Japanese people buy gold and—"

"Stop! You don't need to prove your stupidity to me."

"But—"

"All I know is that you spent two hundred rupees, maybe three, on the necklace."

"Nine," he said, vastly exaggerating the price.

"All right, nine hundred. But what about the rest of the money?"

"You have it!"

"I have nothing!"

He shook his head and turned away.

"Look at me, Sonalal! I'll tell you what you spent it on. What you always spend our money on. Liquor and whores!"

He kept quiet.

"Sona," she said in a voice suddenly soft and sad, "I gave you another chance. A chance to have your family back. Instead, you chose what you've always chosen: liquor and whores!"

He stared at the floor.

———————————

He considered returning to work—if only to recover his old life, measly as it now seemed. But he didn't think he could go back to Humayun's Tomb and charm the way he once had. The tomb was just about the only place in the world where he was still famous. If he went back, he feared he'd prove himself no more than an ordinary charmer—just as Laloo the magician said he was. Once, just once, the gods had let him pipe their own heavenly music, but would they again? And at what cost? Last time he'd lost his beloved Raju. There was no telling what would happen this time. And if the gods didn't bestow their favor—if he played the humdrum music every other charmer played—then people would walk away disappointed, or laugh and say he'd just gotten famous for pulling a foolish stunt. People were that way, exactly that way. No, he couldn't go back.

The trouble was he had no other skill. The only other thing he could possibly do was perform manual labor. Maybe not even that. Every day, he was getting closer to life's exit; he felt the changes in his bones. Was his back strong enough to carry bags of cement or even rice? He doubted it. Too much sitting around, waiting for buses.

He went to the closet. Since he'd smashed his new *been* after Raju died, he looked over several old instruments. Finally, he chose one. With much anxiety, he puckered his lips, then played a few notes. They sounded shrill. He was playing no better than a thousand other charmers, possibly worse. One by one, he picked up the other *beens* and played, trying to will and coax the music. Everything sounded rotten. He was stricken by an awful fear. Had he lost his talent? Could he really be such a dreadful charmer? It crossed his mind that the new *been* he'd destroyed might have possessed magical properties. After giving further thought to this hypothesis, he dismissed it as absurd.

He lifted his *dhoti* and examined his legs, wondering if they could pedal a cycle rikshaw. But though he flexed his legs every which way, he scarcely saw any muscles, certainly not the kind he'd noticed in the vein-engorged legs of *rikshawalas*. Imagine trying to pedal a fat *lala* up a hill with these scrawny legs!

But he had to do something.

11

SONALAL'S MIND was soon diverted from the need to find work. Only a few weeks had passed since he'd gotten rid of the bitter taste in his mouth when suddenly a new problem arose that also happened to be oral. Now his teeth and tongue weren't getting along. More than a dozen times a day, he cried out from pain as his incisors attacked his tongue.

He often spat saliva tinged with blood. He couldn't sleep for fear of waking up and finding his tongue next to him in a puddle of blood.

On those sleepless nights, at first he sought comfort under the banyan tree, which had done what no doctor could for his bitter taste. But this time the tree was indifferent to his plight. One night, when his tongue was throbbing from wounds inflicted by his teeth, he screamed at the callous tree: "What's happening to me?"

He glared at the tree as if expecting an answer. But with its limbs branching one after another, the banyan seemed to juggle the question and transform it into thousands, all ending in an impenetrable maze of leaves. Could it really be so complicated?

In frustration, Sonalal kicked the fiendish tree, then cried out in pain. He limped home. The pain in his foot temporarily offset the pain in his tongue, and he managed to get an hour of sleep.

From the next morning, Sonalal began going around with his mouth partly open.

"You look quite ridiculous," Sarita observed.

He knew he looked ridiculous, and keeping his mouth open also made his jaw ache horribly. But he had to somehow separate his teeth from his tongue. He considered seeing a doctor. Then he asked himself, to what use? A doctor was likely to say the same thing: guilt. Yet this time he was quite sure it was something else.

Soon the spasm from constantly keeping his mouth open became unbearable. His lower jaw felt like it would collapse due to the pressure. But whenever he relaxed his jaw, his teeth would lacerate his tongue again, bringing tears to his eyes.

He was miserable. With no other option, one afternoon he showed up at Dr. Basu's office.

"Dr. Basu is on vacation in Simla," said the doctor's secretary. "He'll be back in two weeks."

Sonalal frowned. "I suppose anyone bitten by a poisonous snake during that time should just pray."

When he stepped back into the afternoon sun, Sonalal had no idea where to go next. What doctor knew how to treat this kind of problem? None. He would just slowly bleed to death from his wounded tongue. As if celebrating their victory, over the next hour his sadistic teeth chopped his tongue four times. Sonalal was so desperate he entertained last resorts.

Even the last of last resorts.

So, late that afternoon, with feelings that couldn't have been more mixed, he rode the bus to Chandni Chowk to see Doctor Seth, the man who thought time could go backward.

Independence Day was near, and the sky over Chandni Chowk was filled with dancing kites of every color. As Sonalal made his way through the old city, he couldn't resist an urge to visit Reena—to partake of what had by now turned into a very pleasurable ritual in their unending quest to cure him of impotence. He detoured in the direction of the brothel. But the prospect of seeing Reena caused him to drop his guard—relax his jaw. His teeth seized the opportunity and viciously stabbed his tongue. He tasted blood.

Sonalal turned around and ran to Doctor Seth's.

As before, the doctor's assistant answered the door. "You again! Why are you back? The doctor isn't in. Go away!"

"I must see Doctor Seth."

"He isn't here, I said!"

The commotion brought the doctor to the door. "What is going on?"

Then Doctor Seth recognized Sonalal. His eyebrows arched as high as they possibly could, but he said nothing. He just gestured for Sonalal to follow him into his office.

Doctor Seth sat down behind his desk and folded his hands. Sonalal remained standing. He felt ashamed—for spitting at the doctor last time and, even more, for coming back.

"Sit down," said Doctor Seth.

Sonalal sat.

Doctor Seth stared at him through narrowed eyes. "Hmm . . ." was all he said.

Sonalal couldn't meet the doctor's gaze. So he looked at the wall, his eyes following branching cracks in the sickly green paint. After a few minutes had passed, Doctor Seth broke the silence.

"So you want to bite your tongue off?"

Sonalal's eyes widened. All of a sudden he was in awe of the great clinician before him.

"Guilt," said Doctor Seth. "That's what it is. First-degree guilt."

"But how? I—"

"Your guilt is wider than the Milky Way, denser than a black hole. What makes you think sitting under a tree will make so much guilt go away?"

"How did you know about the banyan?"

"Never mind that."

"The tree worked last time."

"It didn't! Don't you see? That's why you're here."

"Then what is the solution?"

"There's only one, actually."

"Yes?"

Doctor Seth leaned forward. "You see, pain demands pain. Always. And in greater amount. Twice the original pain multiplied by pi. Now, let's calculate. You committed murder. . . ." Doctor Seth knit his brow, appeared to be concentrating. "This is a hard one. Then again, the precise amount doesn't matter in this case. The most you can do is equal the original. Right?"

Sonalal had grasped the gist. "You don't mean I must—"

"No, I guess you're right. Though it's what you deserve, I must agree that suicide defeats the purpose. Then perhaps the best you can do is get rid of half the guilt."

"At least that's something. Maybe I can live with the other half."

"Maybe you can, maybe not."

Sonalal's teeth snapped his tongue, and he cried out in pain. With moist eyes, he said, "I can't go on like this! Something must be done!"

"There is a price."

"What?"

Doctor Seth pointed to the signboard indicating his consultation fee and looked away. "Pay me thirty rupees from last time and thirty for this time. Sixty total."

Sonalal had brought money, though not that much. He fished into his shirt pocket. Except for loose change, which he kept for the return bus fare, he laid everything on the doctor's desk. The sum came to thirty-eight rupees.

Doctor Seth snatched the money unbecomingly. Then he got up, went to his bookcase, and opened the glass doors. With a faraway look in his eyes, he said, "I stand on the shoulders of giants."

That remark put all kinds of improbable scenarios into Sonalal's head. Before he could sort through them, Doctor Seth pulled a tattered volume from the bookcase and waved it in Sonalal's face.

"This is Nietzsche," the doctor said. "Nietzsche teaches that you must live dangerously and die at the right time."

That sounded interesting to Sonalal, though he thought the doctor ought to explain better. "What does it mean?"

"Nietzsche says there are masters and slaves. You must face your fears—your guilt—all by yourself, or you'll always be a slave."

Sonalal wasn't impressed. He thought this Nietzsche fellow must be one of those touch-me-not high-caste types always looking for an excuse to point to the inferiority of everyone else.

"Do you understand?"

Sonalal looked at least as puzzled as he felt.

"Maybe you don't," said Doctor Seth. "Let me explain it another way, then. Somewhere it's written—one of the *Tantras*, I think—that just as by passion we are bound, so too by passion we are released. Does that make sense to you?"

At first, Sonalal was even more confused. Then it occurred to him the doctor might be referring to his lost manhood, so perhaps what he was saying made a little sense after all—though the precise nature of Doctor Seth's recommendation remained far from clear.

"I think so," Sonalal finally said.

"Good," replied Doctor Seth. "Now, listen. This is the treatment. You are to bite your tongue as hard as you can. And keep biting until you are no longer able."

For thirty-eight rupees, this was the kind of advice that might have prompted Sonalal to spit once more in Doctor Seth's face. But the genius of a doctor had already risen from his chair and stepped well out of spitting range.

"Go!" said Doctor Seth in a voice so authoritative that Sonalal got up and left.

————————————

Sonalal was wretched enough to give anything a try, and a few hours of quiet consideration had unveiled a perverse logic in the doctor's advice. Besides, what was there to lose? Well, his tongue. But he was going to lose it anyway—along with his sanity.

So, late that night, after Sarita fell asleep, he locked himself in the bathroom. Then he sat down opposite the toilet and prepared for the exercise in self-mutilation prescribed by Doctor Seth. He was not particularly fond of pain, so it proved very hard to begin.

But begin he did. And with a doggedness that just might have been courage, he kept on. Over and again, he bit his tongue, hour after hour—shaking from pain, filling the bathroom with tears and muffled cries—until he passed out.

When he opened his eyes in the morning, his head was in the toilet. The bathroom floor was was still wet with his tears and sweat. Amazingly, there was no blood.

He couldn't eat, couldn't talk. Most of all, he couldn't listen to Sarita's endless questions about what had happened. His silence only made her persist.

"Are you really dumb?" she asked one afternoon. "Or just mad? Or have you joined some cult and taken a vow of silence? No, you don't have the character to keep any vows—I know that. This is just some strange ploy of yours, Sona. Don't think I can't see through it. A way to avoid working. As far as I'm concerned, even if you are dumb, you must feed your children. A mute charmer can still play a *been*. And a mute husband is better than a talking one. . . ."

Despite the awful pain in his mouth, he left the house. Over the next few days, he roamed all around Delhi—through crowded bazaars, over the yellow lawns near India Gate, around statues of great men whose heads were decorated with pigeon shit, past big government buildings that resembled tombs of medieval princes. He derived the greatest comfort from circling the huge rotary of Connaught Circle— oblivious to the shops, the hawkers, the shoeshiners, the well-dressed shoppers, the noise, the traffic. His peace of mind increased with every circle: He was on a pilgrimage to some holy place. One day, he made so many circles he felt like he was flying—soaring above the highest clouds, destined for somewhere beyond the follies and miseries of men. Afterward, he wondered if this was the kind of state achieved by ascetics meditating in icy caves on Himalayan mountain peaks.

During those days, he didn't speak to anybody. Apart from water and lukewarm tea, nothing went into his stomach. He came home late at night when Sarita and the boys were asleep and left before they woke up. With all that walking and no food, he lost over a pound a day. And after he'd led this monkish existence for nearly a week, his teeth and tongue were forever reconciled.

12

_____

S ONALAL DIDN'T really appreciate how much he had relished the
solitude of suffering until it became clear most of his problems
remained unsolved. He was still impotent, he still needed work, he
still couldn't bring himself to do the only work he knew, and he was
still married to a woman he wanted to escape from. Worst of all, he
knew he'd once played for the heavens and feared he'd never be
granted an audience again. He estimated he would live another fifteen
years or so, and a dozen times each day for those fifteen years, he'd
remind himself of past glory unattainable forevermore. That is, if he
didn't kill himself. Somewhere he'd heard that's what great musicians
and artists do when their talent dwindles.

His thoughts increasingly returned to his last conversation with
Laloo the magician. He worried Laloo was right: Maybe his music that
had stirred the gods had just been a matter of luck. After all, luck has
to happen to someone, sometime. Even an idiot is capable of an inspired moment.

But during calmer periods, he was sure it wasn't simply luck, the
whim of some mischievous god. He'd heard it said that if a thousand
talking parrots talked for a thousand years, they still couldn't come
up with Gabbar Singh's dialogues in the film _Sholay_. And the same

with the music he'd played that night. It had required a rare talent. He wondered if Ravi Shankar or Bismillah Khan had ever reached such heights. He doubted it. Perhaps nobody had ever played so well. No, not luck at all. And to prove it, he'd do it again. If he could just play that heavenly music one more time, nobody would think it was just a fluke—like winning the lottery. But how to rekindle his talent?

Magic.

Of course! Hadn't Laloo said magicians could smell the ether that flows through the universe? Hadn't Laloo said magicians knew how to contact the highest spirits at will? If only he could learn some of Laloo's skills, then maybe, just maybe, he'd once again be able to play notes that could penetrate the heavens. And if Raju was up there dancing for the gods as Jagat had said, surely Raju would recognize the music. And that music would tell Raju how repentant his father was, how he suffered for his sin, how he missed his favorite son.

———————————

And so, when Sonalal went back to Humayun's Tomb after his long absence, it was not to charm, but to look for Laloo: to learn magic.

He found Laloo playing rummy with the man who sold ice-cold water for ten paisa a glass. All the money was on Laloo's side, and the cold-water man looked very suspicious.

"I should know better than to play cards with magicians," said the cold-water man.

Laloo didn't like the insinuation. "Maybe you should just learn how to play."

That comment immediately ended the game. Sonalal was afraid it would go further—come to blows. But Laloo was big, and when he stood up, chest expanded, the cold-water man just stomped off.

Laloo counted his earnings and grinned. "With all this money," Laloo hollered in the direction the cold-water man had gone, "I'd like a hundred glasses of cold water!"

Laloo erupted into laughter and then shouted, "Make that a thousand glasses! Ice cold, you hear! Ice cold!"

Laloo turned to Sonalal. "You know what that fellow tells people on hot days? He says that when baby gods cry, their tears freeze and turn into ice—something like that. And he claims the water he sells is cooled by the tears of baby gods. Can you believe it—acting like a priest who distributes holy water!"

"Surely no one believes him."

"People believe anything."

They talked some more about the cold-water man.

"It should be illegal to make a living off selling water," said Laloo.

Sonalal nodded. "The government bans all the wrong things."

Eventually there was nothing left to say about water or the cold-water man, and Sonalal told Laloo why he'd come.

"You want to become a magician?"

"Well, not quite—"

"Why?"

Sonalal didn't want to explain that he hoped to reach Raju in heaven—or, at the very least, learn a spell that might help him recover his manhood. So in the end, he opted for brevity. "To help my music."

"Hmm," said Laloo. "Didn't you tell me the spirits had already spoken to you?"

Sonalal shook his head. "No, Laloo *bhai*. They didn't speak. They just listened. Once—only once. I don't know how to make it happen again. I'm afraid I can't. Maybe if I learn some magic . . ."

"Hmmmm."

"What does that mean?"

"Nothing. But if you are free, you might want to come along with me to the next monthly gathering."

"Of whom?"

"Magicians from different parts of Delhi."

"What do you do?"

"Come and see. Next Thursday night, all right?"

———————————

The room was lit by ancient lanterns that had once illuminated a Himalayan shrine now inaccessible due to avalanches. Laloo was sitting on the floor at the front, his legs crossed. Lying on the ground before him was an intricately patterned rug on which were arrayed three silver daggers, a silk wrap with dozens of mantras stitched into it, and a conch shell said to have been used by Lord Indra himself to summon lesser gods.

Laloo raised his hands, and everyone became silent. "Bow before the great Lord Indra, Master of Magicians," said Laloo.

All the magicians bowed. Then Laloo called the gathering to order. "Are there any matters for discussion?"

A youthful magician stood up and said, "I've been having trouble with the incantation for growing a seed into a mango tree in three minutes. It's taking at least ten minutes, sometimes as much as twenty. People just don't have that kind of patience anymore. Maybe I'm doing it wrong. Could someone please tell me the precise spell?"

Everyone seemed to know.

"*Mantru, mantru,*" said one magician.

"*Krim, krum, krim,*" said another.

"*Hrim, vrim, srim,*" said a third.

A heated debate followed. Soon the group divided into three camps, the largest being in favor of "*Krim, krum, krim,*" though "*Mantru, mantru*" had strong support too.

Then someone pulled out a book of Tantric incantations. A solution seemed imminent. But, of the dozen or so magicians present, only one could read, and the book was written in a language he was unfamiliar with.

"I think the book is in Assamese," said the literate magician. "Or perhaps a Naga dialect. Some of them are very obscure."

"It could be Hindi for all we know," said Laloo. "Maybe you don't know how to read either!"

Laughter drowned out the literate magician's protests.

When the group finally quieted down, Laloo said, "This is my friend, the famous Sonalal."

He motioned toward Sonalal, who was sitting in the far corner of the room.

Sonalal acknowledged the magicians with a polite smile and nod. A few of the magicians nodded back, though no one seemed to know why Sonalal was famous.

"You all remember him, don't you?" said Laloo. "The charmer who bit his snake last month—at the start of the Games."

Sonalal didn't like Laloo's mentioning that. He was glad most people had forgotten what happened. In fact, he wished everyone would, for he himself wanted to forget.

But now that the magicians had been reminded, a murmur spread through the room. Many rose to shake Sonalal's hand. In less than a minute, his back was slapped eight times.

Laloo tried to speak over the commotion. "He wants to learn a little magic. . . ."

But the gathering was already out of hand. Someone lit a hookah. A vat of illicit brew made its way around the room.

Laloo came up to Sonalal, smiling. "It always ends like this. But today it happened a bit early."

Sonalal imbibed the tasty brew, shared the hookah. The effect was quite different from what he was used to drinking and smoking. It made him pleasantly dizzy and pulled an emerald veil over his world. Thoughts of cosmic import circulated in his head. Ideas darted out in a thousand directions searching for someplace to settle. They found none. Eventually all his thoughts vanished, and only snakes were left—crawling around in a huge circle, biting each other's tails. He caught a whiff of a novel and very enjoyable aroma. He wondered if it was benzene.

"The ether is good today," said one of the older magicians.

Everyone laughed, Sonalal too. Soon he was laughing hard for no reason at all. He became aware of every sensation in his body, all pleasurable. If he could just be with Reena in this state—rather, if she would do certain things to him while he felt like this—then all the suffering in life would be justified. Or so he thought for seven or eight minutes—before he became nauseated and his head started to feel like a knife was trying to carve its way out.

The magicians drank tea as if it were a religious requirement. The hotter it was outside, the more steaming tea they drank. Their favorite haunt was Dhanu's tea stall, where Dhanu claimed that, after five generations and a million cups, he was on the verge of concocting the perfect cup of tea. But Sonalal didn't care much for Dhanu's milky, sugary brew. It had a metallic taste, and Sonalal could swallow no more than two cups back to back. This occasionally resulted in a little tension with Laloo, who could waste the whole day guzzling one cup after another.

Early one afternoon, after Laloo had emptied his sixth cup and seemed intent on drinking more, Sonalal said, "Laloo *bhai*, by now your blood must be tea!"

"That and liquor," muttered a man sitting in the corner of the tea stall. "Don't forget liquor. Laloo loves liquor more than women."

Although Laloo poked fun at everyone, he generally couldn't take it, and Sonalal expected him to respond with a caustic earful. But Laloo just smiled deferentially at the man.

The man was so old he could have been any age. His face was intricately lined, and when he grinned, only a single dark brown tooth could be seen. His eyes were no longer clear; he might have been blind.

"Who is he?" Sonalal whispered to Laloo.

"He's Ratan the Great, the oldest man in India—almost two hundred. He is descended from Bir Das, Jahangir's court magician. Ratan the Great is the only one alive who has successfully performed the rope trick."

"The rope trick?"

"You know, *the* rope trick—make a rope rise high into the sky all by itself, then climb to the top of it."

"Can it really be done?"

Laloo turned to Ratan the Great and said, "Baba, he doesn't believe in the rope trick."

"Who is this doubter?"

"Sonalal, Baba. He's with us these days, but he's also a charmer, a very famous one. He bit a snake."

Sonalal flashed Laloo an angry glare, for he'd told him to stop reminding people of the incident.

"I heard about that," said Ratan the Great. "Frankly, I couldn't understand what all the fuss was about. The snake had no venom in it. A harmless creature, right?"

Sonalal looked away.

"So tell me then, what was so incredible?"

Sonalal kept quiet.

"Now the rope trick *is* incredible," continued the old man, "so incredible it scared the queen of England in the last century. She nearly went mad worrying about it. If Indians climbed to the top of ropes standing in the air, then Indian heads would be higher than English heads—or so the queen feared. The masters would always be looking up at the slaves. That was bad enough. But since no one can spit with the accuracy of an Indian, the queen was even more afraid all those Indians would spit on the heads of her officers and soldiers. The whole Raj would fall apart. So she sent a man named Major Banks to find out if the rope trick was real. I must have climbed for him over a hundred times—once even took him up with me! Oh, he believed it. But Banks also understood how women think. When he went back, he told the queen the rope trick couldn't be done. So England held on to India. If he'd just told the truth, we'd have been independent long before Gandhi."

"Can you do the rope trick now?" asked Sonalal.

"To do it, you have to be able to see, and I've been blind for thirty years. But a strange thing is happening to me. I've become so old, I think I'm starting to get younger. Who knows, maybe one day I'll see again."

"There must be someone—"

"There's no one else," said Ratan the Great. "That's why what the queen feared could never have happened. Even in those days, when the ether flowed freely, and people were levitating wherever you looked, only two or three others could do the rope trick. You see, real magic is expensive. Today there's nobody in India willing to pay its price."

"What price?" asked Sonalal.

"The price great magicians have always had to pay."

"And what is that?"

"Penance, penance, more penance! You can't smell the cosmic ether just like that. Greatness only comes to those who suffer. And these fellows who call themselves magicians, well, putting the ace of spades in someone's pocket from ten feet away isn't quite the same thing as transposing people's heads, is it?"

13

RATAN THE GREAT was right. In the company of Laloo and other magicians, Sonalal heard a lot about the union of the male and female principles that constitute reality, about mystical communion with the *shakti* that controls the universe, about the need to constantly renew one's magic by cultivating divine favor. But all told, had he witnessed any magic—real magic? Everything he saw turned out to be a two-headed coin. The man buried alive had a secret breathing tube. The so-called volunteer in the crowd was planted. All transformations depended on drapes, smoke, secret compartments, mirrors. More disappointing were the half-dozen spells said to enhance sexual prowess, which Sonalal recited every time he visited Reena. Then she would patiently caress, tickle, kiss, nibble, and massage his various parts—which gave him immense gratification but did not produce the intended outcome.

And so, the days passed, slowly. The more Sonalal listened and observed, the more the magicians seemed as bound by the laws of nature as everyone else—maybe more so. Of course, Laloo didn't see it that way. Late one morning, after he had just pulled larger and larger balls out of his mouth—his favorite trick—Laloo grinned widely before the crowd and announced, "You've just witnessed a man penetrate the veil of Maya."

The crowd clapped enthusiastically. Laloo took six or seven bows, acting like he'd just returned from the moon.

It was all a bit too much for Sonalal, though he did his best to hide his sentiments. Being no stranger to the world of roadside performers, he told himself things had to be this way. In the street, like most places, talk counts much more than talent. Thousands can make a cobra come out of a basket, yet so few can really charm. How many times had he told himself there was only one genuine charmer in all Delhi?

The crowd soon dispersed. Only he and Laloo were left.

"They always like that trick," said Laloo, as he counted his earnings. "There's nothing like magic. Nothing. What do you think, charmer *sahib*?"

Sonalal rolled his eyes but was glad Laloo didn't notice. Now he realized he'd never find what he needed here. If this was magic, it wasn't the kind he was after. But he wasn't ready to leave this new world just yet, for he'd developed quite a fondness for his *jadugar* friends. And although their knowledge of magic might be debatable, they certainly knew lots of dirty jokes. Sonalal especially liked the countless variations of the one about Bindu, the moneylender's lustful daughter, said to possess "a face like Hema Malini, eyes like Sharmila Tagore, a waist like Waheeda Rehman, and hips like Rekha."

With all the diversion, there were periods when Sonalal almost forgot why he'd sought the magicians in the first place. This did him more good than any magic could have. And during those weeks, he did learn a few things—like how to lie with an innocent face, an essential skill in this complicated world. If nothing else, it would prove useful in dealing with Sarita, particularly when he came home late from the brothel in Chandni Chowk.

But soon Sonalal was again dogged by the old concerns that had prompted him to seek out Laloo and his kind. Fed up with hyperbole, he longed to chat with Ratan the Great. If the old man had indeed done the rope trick, he must know something the others didn't. Maybe Ratan the Great really had sniffed the cosmic ether. Maybe Ratan the Great could tell him how to seduce the magic back into his *been*—and perhaps his loins too.

Wednesday morning in Dhanu's tea stall, Sonalal found the blind magician sitting alone, exploring his left nostril with his little finger. Without asking, Sonalal pulled up a chair and sat down at the table.

"Who is it?"

"Me, Sonalal."

"Ah yes, the snakebiter. I want to talk to you, Sonalal. But first drink some tea. Dhanu's tea is the best in the world."

"I've also been wanting to talk to you."

"Talk then."

Dhanu set another cup of tea on the table. Sonalal took a sip of the tea, which was particularly rotten today. He pushed the cup aside and came straight to the point. "Tell me more about the cosmic ether."

Ratan the Great folded his hands behind his head and looked thoughtful. "The ether is the most amazing thing in the universe. It flows everywhere, connects everything. It can't be seen, but it can be smelled. When a man smells it, he can do whatever magic he pleases."

"Can he make time go backward?"

"Anything!"

Sonalal's eyes widened. "What does it smell like? Benzene?"

"What's that?"

"Never mind," said Sonalal. "What I meant is, does the ether smell like a snake biting its own tail?"

Ratan the Great's blind eyes began to gleam as if they beheld a vision from another world. "The ether smells like—oh, it's very hard to describe. But it's the most wonderful smell that exists."

"Is it like a mango?" asked Sonalal.

"Well . . . hmm . . . maybe. More like an overly ripe mango, though. You know, one of those really soft mangoes with lots of bruises that is on the verge of going rotten. When you slice such a fruit open, a sharp smell vies against the sweetness. But if you forget that the mango is going bad, you realize the two smells are really working together to create a truly marvelous aroma. Do you get what I mean?"

Sonalal tried to imagine what the smell was like, but at that moment it wasn't much easier than imagining the smell of a snake biting its own tail. Could they be one and the same? At least it was possible to find out what a rancid mango smelled like.

"More than anything else in the world," said Sonalal, "I want to learn how to smell the ether. Can you teach me?"

"It's not so simple," replied Ratan the Great. "But we'll discuss that later. Now you must tell me something."

"What?"

A grin crept onto Ratan the Great's face. "I'm finally certain I'm getting younger. This morning I felt the itch for the first time in twenty years—what an incredible feeling!"

"This is true."

Ratan the Great's expression became conspiratorial. He leaned over the table and whispered, "Sonalal, my friend, all the prostitutes I've been with must be long gone. And if any happen to be left, by now they have to be old hags. Just imagine being seduced by a two-hundred-year-old woman! You get my point. But Laloo tells me you've been to every brothel in Delhi. You see, I'm a little scared of embarrassing myself. It's been so long! So I was hoping you could guide me to a woman gentle and patient enough to ease an old man back to youth."

"I'm not quite the man I once was," replied Sonalal. "But yes, I know of a few such women. Tell me one thing, though."

"Yes?"

"Aren't there incantations for this sort of thing—to strengthen one's potency? Haven't you tried them?"

"Tried them all! It's witchcraft, I tell you! For thousands of years, witches have been poisoning our knowledge with spells of no use. And I'm afraid those witches' spells won't help me or anyone else in this matter."

Sonalal nodded knowingly. Then he asked, "What about the ether?"

"When you sniff the ether, you have no need for women. But even I'm not able to smell the ether all that easily these days. Now tell me, will you help or not?"

Sonalal thought hard. After considering nearly three dozen candidate sirens, he said, "You could go to Basanti at the Ajmeri Gate brothel. Or better yet, try Sonia in Daryaganj. The Daryaganj brothel isn't far from the main bus stop. Yes, go to Sonia. She has the patience of a mountain."

"She doesn't look like a mountain, does she?"

"How does it matter to a blind man?"

"A blind man can feel better than most can see."

"You will like the way Sonia feels. And she has the delicate skill of an ant."

"I hope she won't bite!"

"Only gently—in all the right places."

Ratan the Great was profuse in his thanks, and Sonalal hoped the old man might now be willing to divulge a secret or two. But before Sonalal could steer the conversation back to magic, another magician sat down at the table. Then one more came, and everyone began to talk about Hindi films. For a blind man, Ratan the Great knew a lot about films and their stars. The discussion went on and on.

Frustrated, Sonalal excused himself.

As he walked away, an idea seized control of his mind. He crossed the street and went over to a fruit vendor, whose cart was loaded with ripe mangoes. One by one, Sonalal pressed each mango in order to identify the mushiest fruit.

"Stop squishing my mangoes!" shouted the vendor, who had a bushy white beard like a fair-weather cloud. "What's wrong with you anyway?"

"I'll take this one," said Sonalal, holding a soft red mango that felt like it would burst if he gave it another squeeze.

"Just one? After all the damage you've done, you want just one? I'll have to charge you for two."

Sonalal shrugged. "Fine, but slice it up, then."

"I'll have to charge you for that too."

"Then you might as well charge me for looking at your ugly face!"

"That's very funny," said the fruit vendor. "Oh, and by the way, have you ever looked in a mirror, hero *sahib*?"

Sonalal threw a rupee onto the cart, then tromped off. He turned down a side street and walked until he found a shady tree. He sat down under the tree, legs folded, his back against the trunk, and began to contemplate the fruit.

The mango really couldn't be said to be any single color but, like a rainbow, contained shades of all—red, yellow, orange, green, even hints of indigo and violet around the bruised regions. But for the impression his thumb had made, the fruit's smooth egglike shape seemed to capture some essential property of the universe. Sonalal picked up the mango and began to stroke its cool curvaceous surface, caress it. He did this for a long time. Eventually the tension became so great he couldn't hold back any longer. He had to get inside the fruit, sniff it, lap up its sweet nectar.

He thrust his long thumb deep into the fruit. Sticky juice squirted out and ran down his wrist. He licked it up, then inserted his tongue into the hole, sucking the delicious nectar. Then he started to nibble away gently at the ambrosial flesh.

Suddenly he lost all control. He clawed open the whole fruit, then chewed it like a famished animal. His face was soon covered with bits of yellow-orange flesh. Warm sticky juice dripped from his chin and ears.

The mango was finished. But Sonalal quickly realized that he wasn't. For he now felt a pressure beneath his *dhoti* that was stronger than any even Reena had been able to induce. Such potential! If he could somehow harness this, take it to Reena right away, he was certain he'd have his manhood back in ten minutes or less. But Reena was nowhere near, and with this realization he sensed his erection beginning to wane. He couldn't afford to lose this one—for all he knew, it might be his last real chance.

It occurred to him that maybe he could help himself. He glanced around. He wasn't in exactly the most secluded of places. But still . . .

Just then, a group of schoolboys walked by, engaged in a heated discussion about a cricket match—India versus someone or other. He waited for them to pass. But by the time the boys' voices could no longer be heard, Sonalal realized there was nothing left to work with.

He now became aware of an irritating stickiness all over his face. On the ground in front of him, flies hovered above the mango peel, which suddenly seemed no different from all the other filth that lay in stinking gutters and garbage heaps. Sure, it had smelled and tasted good, but was it really so great? He could barely even remember the smell now, and what he did recall was on the sharp side. As Sonalal batted flies away from his face and continued to stare at what was left of the mango, he became depressed. He wondered if Ratan the Great had made up the whole thing about the ether and mangoes.

Desperate for answers, Sonalal went searching for Laloo. But Laloo was nowhere to be found. Someone said Laloo had been drinking late into the night, and who knew if he'd be coming at all today?

In the afternoon, Laloo finally showed up, eyes bloodshot. Without so much as a greeting, Sonalal pointed to the magician's bag slung over Laloo's shoulder and asked outright, "Do you know any magic?"

"What do you mean?"

"Well, you do this and that, and you say it's all magic. Is any of it genuine?"

"All of it," said Laloo, grinning mischievously. "There is magic everywhere."

It was hot. Sweat was streaming down Sonalal's face. He had no patience for magician-talk.

"Tell me straight, Laloo."

Laloo didn't speak for a long while. A wistful expression gradually came over his face, and his eyes turned glassy. At last he said, "I know what you mean."

"And?"

"I too used to be preoccupied with this question. Of course, I was much younger then. Now it doesn't seem to matter."

"You're a magician, and you don't care whether there's such a thing as magic?"

"Not so much."

"But—"

"You're right, though. Nothing I do is magic—just silly tricks."

"Then it's all lies?"

"There is a lot of truth in lies."

Sonalal frowned. "You make so light of cheating people!"

"We don't cheat. Sometimes we dupe, though."

"Cheat, dupe—what's the difference?"

"People don't pay to be cheated. Some pay to be duped. I'm sure it's the same with charming."

Sonalal ignored the gibe. "But do you believe real magic is possible?"

"Once I saw a yogi," said Laloo, "a genuine yogi who'd suffered many years of self-mortification. He did amazing things which even I, a magician familiar with two thousand years of tricks, cannot explain. And there are countless accounts of Tantrics with tremendous powers. Such as Bhubru Baba, who lives on one of the mountains near Nepal. With a single incantation, they say, the great Baba can turn a Bengal tiger into a puddle of milk. And of course, there is the story of Jahangir's court magician, Bir Das—an ancestor of Ratan the Great. It is documented in court records that Bir Das made the emperor's favorite dog float up to the top of the palace ceiling. Next, he cast a spell, and the dog's head and tail dropped off. Then the rest of the dog's body came crashing down. The horrified emperor commanded Bir Das to bring the royal dog back to life. Bir Das just smiled, then rejoined the dog's head and tail to the body. After that, he set the dead animal on fire. When the dog's body had burned to ashes, Bir Das uttered a long mantra, and suddenly the dog jumped out of the fire and right into the arms of the overjoyed emperor!"

Sonalal had heard that story before and liked hearing it again. He'd saved Raju's ashes and all along had harbored a secret hope of resurrecting his beloved cobra—just as Bir Das had resurrected the emperor's dog. Then, not only would he have Raju back, but Rani would no longer hunt him. And maybe he'd even be able to make the gods listen to his music again. Maybe only Raju, with his exquisitely fine ear for music, could coax him to play that way. Perhaps it was even simpler than that. Maybe he just had to love his snake as much as he loved Raju. But he knew that could never happen again.

"What was the mantra Bir Das used?"

"For more than four hundred years," said Laloo, "every magician in India has wanted the answer to that question."

14

SONALAL'S CHAT with Laloo left him in an odd mood. In a world where magicians themselves were unsure of magic, the veil of Maya that hid reality seemed more opaque than ever. What chance did he have of penetrating it? Ether, rotten mangoes, benzene, snakes biting their own tails: What did it all mean? Did it mean anything? And how to know? Suddenly Sonalal felt very lonely. He longed for Reena and Jagat, the only people he fully trusted.

He found Jagat at his usual spot in front of the tomb, chewing a *paan* and waiting for the next bus.

"Ah, there's the great magician," said Jagat. "P. C. Sorcar himself! Oh, magnificent one, please don't turn me into a dung heap!"

"Stop it, Jagat *bhai!*"

Jagat spit *paan* juice onto the road. The burnt-orange liquid glistened in the sunlight as both men contemplated the latest contribution to the local calligraphy.

"Tell me then," said Jagat, "what are you doing with those tricksters?"

"A good question."

"Why do you need to learn tricks? Is magic really so hard to find, Sona?"

"Yes."

"Just look at that bird!" Jagat pointed to a fat crow scavenging the gutter. "What is a plane but a poor imitation of that creature?"

Sonalal stared at the crow as it pecked out the last few kernels from a filthy corncob, then headed for a rotting banana peel.

"The plane looks like an improvement to me," said Sonalal.

Jagat shook his head. "Forget the bird. You know what I mean. Your magician friends are right about Maya's veil. Only the veil isn't over the world, it's over their eyes. Your eyes! You must lift the veil, Sona—see the way you used to."

Sonalal smiled patronizingly. "I wish it were that simple, Jagat *bhai*."

"Perhaps it isn't. I do not know much about these things. And unlike you, I don't torture myself over them. I will keep living day after day, just as I already have, and then one day it will be over. I'm not sure there's anything more than that. Are you?"

"There must be!"

Jagat made a dismissive gesture with his hands. "Well, if there is, I don't understand how pulling a pigeon out from under your turban will help you find it."

"That is true."

"Then?"

"Then what?"

Both became quiet. A truck's brakes screeched somewhere in the distance.

Finally Sonalal said, "I have to play great music again, Jagat *bhai*. Let them keep my manhood, but I must get my music back. If Raju is up there—just as you once said—then maybe I can reach him if I am able to play like I once did. It's my only hope of telling him how sorry I am, how much I love him, how much I miss—"

"But Sona, I really don't know if Raju is up there."

"*I know!* I'm sure of it. That's why I must learn to play great music again. Sometimes I think the only way to find my music is to go far away where there are no distractions—maybe some secluded ashram— where it's so quiet I can hear the gods breathe. Then I'll play and play until the gods let me know my music is right again."

"For a man as unholy as yourself, you seem to be placing a lot of hope on the concern of gods."

Sonalal's brow became almost as wrinkled as his *kurta,* but he said nothing.

"And the distractions you speak of," continued Jagat, "are life itself. The reason you are the best charmer I've ever heard is because your music makes me feel that living and everything that goes with it, the things you call distractions—wives and children, coughs and colds, liquor and *beedis,* lotteries, hot boring days, charming itself— are important in some way. Sona, you need those distractions. You must put every one of them into your music."

"What you say sounds very good, Jagat *bhai,* and maybe it was once even true. But nothing is like it used to be. These days the only thing all those distractions do for me is distract."

Over the ensuing weeks, Jagat's frequent pestering made it easier for Sonalal to gradually distance himself from the magicians. He stopped going to their gatherings. He went back to his old tea stall, where the tea now tasted heavenly. And he did his best to avoid Laloo.

But when they did cross paths, he could tell Laloo was hurt. One afternoon, Sonalal tried to explain.

"It's just that I was looking for a way to put magic back into my music," he said, "play my *been* like I did the night—"

"Who ever heard of someone creating magic by blowing into a dried-out pumpkin?" interrupted Laloo. "Isn't that what a *been* is—a dried-out pumpkin?"

Before Sonalal could decide whether to shrug off the remark or get upset, Laloo added, "Look! Here comes another master magician— your brother, the cold-water man, carting around the frozen tears of baby gods!"

That was too much for Sonalal. He scowled at Laloo and left.

After calming down, Sonalal decided he still wanted to reconcile. But over the next few days, whenever he made overtures, Laloo answered with one biting comment or another.

Eventually Sonalal just gave up.

In secret, he tried to reproduce the great music he'd once played. He would wait until his sons were at school and Sarita was at the market, then take out his *been*. But the music wouldn't come. The notes sounded dull, flat, clunky, commonplace—like they were being produced by a dried-out pumpkin. There was no pain in his happy melodies, no hope in his sad melodies. Simple tunes sounded all too simple, complex ones unnecessarily complicated. His music hung in the hot muggy air as if it had no place to go—as if no place in the universe would accept it. There were moments he was absolutely convinced he'd lost all his talent—a peacock plucked of his plumes. Was there anything to live for?

But at other times, he decided he was being too harsh on himself. After all, he hadn't played in quite a while. It had taken decades of daily practice to learn to play the way he once did. Why shouldn't it take a little practice to play that way again?

So he practiced. And practiced. But although his knuckles became stiff, his music still sounded no good.

He became so frustrated he once again chased after otherworldly solutions. Through fervent prayer, he attempted to secure the favor of goddesses of art and fortune. He made pilgrimages to shrines where dancing statues were said to actually dance, where all sorts of miraculous transformations had been reported: dirt to gold, water to honey, blind to visionary. But his music did not transform.

What would it take? Whatever it was, he'd do it.

So he sought counsel from the wise. Since Delhi was full of such people, he got lots of advice. With complete sincerity, he followed it all. He took the spice out of his food. He meditated, fasted. He let a guru who said he came from high in the Himalayas walk all over him. He even let an exorcist whack him with a bamboo stick. Because he believed he deserved the pain, he begged for another beating.

But it had no effect on his music. Nothing did.

Day by day, his gloom grew. It looked like he'd never be able to communicate with Raju. And without that, life seemed to have no purpose. Soon he was so desperate he began to succumb to overtures from the netherworld. In the middle of the night, when his anxieties knew no bounds, he negotiated with frightening demons. "I'll do anything," he promised. "Anything! Just give me back my music!"

The wicked creatures didn't keep their bargain. The demons ran off with Sonalal's soul, but his music remained uninspired—uninspiring. No cobra worth speaking of would dance for this. And the gods would just laugh. Or even strike him down with a thunderbolt for having such pretentions but no talent.

One afternoon, Sonalal was kicking small rocks in the area outside the tomb. Over the past hour, he had cursed just about everything: the rocks, the heat, life itself.

Jagat was watching. Eventually he went up to Sonalal and said, "If you keep kicking rocks like that, you'll have the toes of a leper."

"Just as well. I feel like one."

Jagat frowned, then wiped his forehead. "Sona, you must get back to charming."

Sonalal laughed bitterly and kicked another rock.

"We miss you, Sona. I miss you."

Sonalal rested his hand affectionately on Jagat's shoulder.

"For how many years have we been together?" asked Jagat.

"At least ten."

"Twelve, Sona. Twelve. Maybe it's a sad thing to say, but I know you better than I ever knew my poor wife."

Just then, the cold-water man passed by with his cart of divinely cooled water. Both men watched quietly until the cold-water man disappeared.

Sonalal finally broke the silence. "It is not easy for me either, Jagat *bhai*. But it's even harder to come back."

"You must not let all this craziness confuse you so much. Maybe you should look at the tomb."

Jagat motioned toward the tomb as if Sonalal needed to be shown where it was. Sonalal shrugged.

"Sitting here day after day for so many years," said Jagat, "it is easy to forget."

"Forget what? This tomb is no different from Safdarjang's Tomb and dozens of other tombs, forts, and gates scattered all over Delhi."

"No, Sona, it's a great tomb, all the more special because it's the tomb of Akbar's father and was constructed during Akbar's reign."

"As if I don't—"

"Think of that, Sona. Akbar! Akbar the Great—greatest emperor since Asoka! You are right that Delhi is littered with reminders of kings and princes. But whom do we remember? Akbar—almost no one else. Who remembers the hundreds of Moghul princes who didn't become emperor? Who remembers the kings of minor kingdoms? Nobody. And you are a prince among charmers, perhaps even a king, but it is a minor kingdom. You are not an emperor, never can be. To be an emperor, there must be an empire. Even if strange things keep happening to you, no one will remember you except possibly a few other charmers, and soon they too will forget."

Sonalal brushed a fly off his ear. "I wouldn't care if the world forgot me, if I could just once play my *been* the way I did that night. If I could get Raju to perform only one dance in heaven—"

"Are you sure?"

"About what?"

Jagat looked Sonalal in the eye and said, "Are you sure you're not missing all the attention?"

Now that Jagat had said it, he wasn't so sure.

"I'm very sure," he said forcefully.

The cold-water man went by again, shouting something about nectar from heaven.

Jagat sneered. "That cold-water fellow must be one of the most irritating men in the world."

"Ask Laloo."

"Another irritating man. Maybe the bastards have the same father."

Sonalal grinned.

Then Jagat said, "You have to go on, even if you fear stumbling. You must find courage."

"You don't understand, Jagat *bhai*. It isn't a matter of courage."

Jagat shook his head. "It's never anything else, Sona. And the kind of courage I'm talking about is much harder than facing an angry king cobra with only your bare hands to defend you."

Sonalal was still thinking about what Jagat had said when a tourist bus arrived. Jagat went off to perform. At first, Sonalal watched with a new kind of interest, almost as if he'd never seen a man charm a snake. But soon it felt all too familiar. The envy of the unemployed set in. He criticized Jagat's talent, his technique. He scolded himself for being so low, so mean. Disgusted, he turned away.

He found himself facing the entrance to the tomb. Though he'd been here nearly every day for over a dozen years, he couldn't recall ever going inside for the specific purpose of looking—just looking. He must have, at least once. But if he had, it hadn't made much of an impression. So now, as the tourists watching Jagat's performance would soon do, Sonalal went in—to view the tomb Haji Begum built in memory of her husband, Emperor Humayun, who died after falling off a ladder.

Once inside, Sonalal was struck as never before by the sheer size of the octagonal structure, its potent geometry, its many symmetries. The double dome and lofty arches, the red sandstone walls inlaid with white and black marble, the intricate stone lattice screens, all combined to create an otherworldly effect. Although from the outside the tomb seemed immovably heavy, inside the place felt light, as if the entire edifice, huge as it was, could fly. Humayun's Tomb was a magnificent place! All this time he'd been sitting in front of the tomb like an idiot—never appreciating what was inside! How blind could he be?

Soon he heard the tramping feet of the tourist group Jagat had just charmed for, its guide chattering facts in Hindi about the Moghul empire and the tomb's architecture. Sonalal found the guide's voice irksome. Couldn't the fellow just let people look? As Sonalal was about to move away from the tourist group, he heard the guide say, "The design of the Taj Mahal was based on Humayun's Tomb." Sonalal didn't know that. Suddenly he had an urge to travel—to explore, escape.

He listened to the rest of the guide's discussion of the Taj, then wandered off on his own. Eventually the tourists left, and it became quiet again. The only sounds were the patting of his sandals on the ground and the faint buzz from beehives high above. In the solitude of red sandstone, what Jagat had said made more and more sense. Akbar had ruled an immense empire. His achievement was so great that, even centuries later, the world still came to admire the big, beautiful stones that commemorated him, his ancestors, his descendants. What had he, Sonalal, done? What could he ever do? He should just get back to living—charming for a living. Even if he made great music again, it would make little difference to anyone. He'd done it once, and no one noticed—except Raju, whom he'd killed. It was just the hysteria about snakebiting that made him think his music mattered. That he mattered. Jagat was right: Nothing he could do would make the world remember him after he was gone. He didn't matter.

But no! He had mattered—if only for a few seconds. What he did was important. Great music mattered. It had to! Even if it fell on deaf ears.

Still, his anxieties had multiplied in the last hour, and he was less sure about mattering than any time since he'd become a murderer. As dusk enveloped the tomb, he also began to feel entombed.

Liquor, he needed liquor. And something else too.

15

*H*E WAS positively garrulous by the time he arrived at the brothel. In the lucidity of inebriation, he was full of insights into the human condition. He shared them with Reena.

"A man and a monkey are the same," he said as he lay on the bed, his head in her lap. "Except for one thing. A man can make moving music, build breathtaking tombs, sculpt sublime statues. . . . Reena, have you seen the sculptures at the Elephanta caves?"

She shook her head.

"Nor have I. But people say they are magnificent! You have to take a boat to get there. And the caves are supposed to be visited by Lord Shiva himself. . . . What about the Taj? You must have been there. No? Me neither. Isn't that a shame? Today I overheard a tour guide talk about the Taj. He said it took twenty thousand workers twenty years to construct it—the most marvelous thing ever created by men. But we'll never see it! And there are so many other things we'll never see. . . ."

He went on, describing the places he'd heard tour guides and tourists at the tomb talk about over the years; he'd seen pictures of many of these places on the postcards Mohan the souvenir seller displayed on his cart. He spoke of the cave paintings at Ajanta, the huge stone temples of Khajuraho, other places. "India is such a great country," he said. "Foreigners see everything in two weeks, but what have we, who've spent our whole lives here, seen?"

Half an hour later, he had moved beyond the borders of India.

"For so many years," he said, "I've been performing for people from faraway places. And I've heard about amazing things. Someone once told me that, in the jungles of South America, there are giant snakes that can eat a man alive! I've always wondered if those snakes could be charmed. If anybody can make them dance, it's me. Of course I'll never get a chance. . . ."

As he emerged from his drunkenness, the afternoon's anxieties returned. "Can you understand what it's like to know greatness for just a moment and then know that, no matter how hard you try, it will never happen again?"

"At least you've known it for a moment," said Reena.

"Hah!"

"Sona, do you think a sunset would seem so wonderful if it lasted forever?"

She had a point, but he was a trifle irritated by the comparison, which seemed too mundane to describe his anguish. Besides, he was no longer in the mood for philosophizing.

"Why don't we go away somewhere?" he said.

His own idea surprised him. Yet it felt right and, a moment later, he was burning with the excitement of escaping from his measly existence. "Come with me, Reena," he said more earnestly.

A sad smile developed on her face. "When I was young," she said, "if a man seemed nice and particularly fond of me, I hoped he'd take me away from here. But though there have been many men, not one has asked me to go away with him—not in the way I wanted."

"I am that man, Reena."

"I wish you were."

He understood what she meant, but he still felt hurt.

"Don't look like that, Sona. I feel more for you than any other customer."

"Customer? I'm more than a customer."

She gently kissed his forehead. "Of course you are. Much more. That's what I meant."

Their eyes met, and he realized that going away wasn't the important part of his plan. It was Reena. And the only way to have her to himself was to escape from Delhi.

"Run away with me, Reena. I—"

"It's too late to run away."

"Well, then let's just go somewhere—for a week or two, that's all."

"It won't be like you hope, Sona. If we were young—"

"You are."

"No. When you first came to me, I was younger than you, but now I am older."

Her words struck him as strange, for Sarita had recently said something similar, although, unlike Reena, she left no doubt as to the cause of her rapid aging.

"Why don't we just go?" he said.

He could tell she was seriously considering the proposal. He hoped she'd decide quickly. All the alcohol had filled his bladder, and he didn't think he could wait much longer.

Finally she said, "Agree to one condition, then."

"What?"

"Love, but no *love*."

He wasn't sure what she meant.

"No lovemaking."

He couldn't have imagined a less appealing condition. Ever since he'd been stricken with impotence, what they'd been doing wasn't exactly what he'd call lovemaking, but whatever it was had been immensely pleasurable—at least for him. And despite so many failed attempts, he still believed that, if anyone could cure him, it was Reena. But now he wondered if she had simply given up hope of restoring his manhood, a thought that filled him with tremendous anxiety.

"But why?" he asked.

She gazed straight at him with liquid eyes and replied, "You, I hope, are the one person I don't have to explain this to."

Now he understood that she didn't want any reminder of this, the life she lived night after night. Though still disappointed, he squeezed her hand. He was embarrassed over what he had to say next. But he had to be honest. "I don't have much money anymore."

"Don't worry," she said. "We will stay in the very best hotel we can find."

"How?"

She pointed to an ancient dresser drawer with a keyhole, then got up. From behind a wall calendar above the dresser, she removed a key. She unlocked the drawer and pulled out a tin toffee box. Inside were gold chains, bangles, and rings.

"Rich men give expensive gifts," she said. "Sometimes I think half the wedding jewelry in Chandni Chowk is in this box. A little of this will go a long way."

He caught the last bus home. On the way, it rained hard. He pressed his face against the window and watched city sights blurred by the downpour.

By the time he got off the bus, the rain had stopped. As he walked home, he slowed down to admire the myriad reflections of streetlights in puddles scattered all over the uneven road. The reflections reminded him of the clay lamps children float on the water during Diwali.

He walked on, fretting over what he'd tell Sarita and the boys. With a little luck, they'd be asleep right now. But he'd have to say something in the morning.

The whole night he stayed awake worrying. Never before had he provoked Sarita as he was about to, with what could be seen only as an act of war. He considered all sorts of explanations—lies. None seemed sufficient. By morning, bits of his fingernails lay scattered throughout his bedsheets, and his cuticles were bleeding.

At breakfast, he waited until everyone was on a second cup of tea before making his announcement. "I have to be away for a while," he said as if he were a soldier called to the front.

It couldn't have sounded better.

Sarita's eyes became icy. "Why?"

He ignored her.

She fired question after question, but he gave no reply.

"Answer me!" she shrieked.

Her words sounded like a whip on a bull's back. But he hadn't come up with a believable story yet. So, without looking at her, he mumbled, "We'll talk about this after the boys leave for school."

That moment arrived much too quickly for his liking.

"Well?" said Sarita, as soon as Ramesh shut the door.

He still hadn't fabricated the kind of brilliant lie the situation demanded. So he thought it best to say no more than necessary to prevent Sarita from castrating him before he left tomorrow.

"Explain!"

"I have to go away," he said matter-of-factly. "That's all."

"That's all? That's all? How can you say that to your wife?"

She narrowed her eyes, stared at him as if he were a spider to crush. He thought it best not to reply.

She grabbed his *kurta* by the collar. He braced for a blow.

"For how long are you going?" she asked, yanking his collar.

"A week, maybe two."

"Where?"

He didn't know yet; Reena was to decide.

"I don't know," he said.

She threw her hands up. "You have to go away. You don't know where. What's going on?"

He considered telling the truth. Although the tactic had worked before, this time he feared she'd believe him.

"I can't explain," he eventually said.

She tightened her lips. She seemed to be thinking, weighing, deciding. At last she said, "Then don't come back."

"I will," he said, as gently as possible, so it didn't sound like a threat.

She opened her mouth as if to scream some insult. But though her mouth remained open, she uttered nothing.

He felt sorry for her—because he was going and, even more, because he was coming back.

16

THE THORNY desert transformed into rugged mountains and then rolling hills. The train slowed, and soon Sonalal and Reena were in the city of lakes, Udaipur. She had booked a room at one of the most famous hotels in India, the Lake Palace.

It took Sonalal a long time to become accustomed to the opulence of the palace-turned-hotel: marble floors, granite pillars, antique furniture, stained-glass windows, so many other things. At times, the air smelled faintly of jasmine, and the sun collaborated with the lake to turn the ivory palace walls shades of pink, blue, and green. Sonalal had never been in such a luxurious place, and at first it seemed too much, making him wonder if he'd come too far from the village he'd been born in. It didn't help that the hotel staff kept staring at him as if he was an illiterate bumpkin. But after Reena paid the first bills and handed out some generous tips, their stares became accepting if somewhat amused, and Sonalal gradually felt more comfortable. As time slowly passed, he began to feel like he was floating through a dream world. And there were moments when, while watching a launch chase the sunset over Lake Pichola, he imagined himself the latest Maharana of Mewar, descendant of the Sun God.

In their room were buttons and gadgets Sonalal wasn't used to.

The bathroom proved especially vexing. He hadn't sat on a Western-style toilet before, though it was one of those things he'd always been curious about. When he finally did sit on it, the experience was anticlimactic. Though he'd never been constipated in his life, his bowels didn't budge for two days. But at last his sphincter became accustomed to the new sight, and the world grew subtle again.

At night, there was usually some kind of entertainment. On their third evening there, everyone gathered for a performance by a local charmer. Rajasthani charmers were supposed to be some of the best, and Sonalal couldn't stay away from the show. But after hearing a few notes, it became clear to him this charmer was an amateur. Sonalal had to restrain himself from snatching the fellow's *been* in the middle of the performance and giving him a lesson.

Everyone else was captivated. A white woman standing next to Sonalal started humming with the music, and then her two daughters, both in their teens, rose to dance. This elicited a smile from the charmer. Perhaps hoping for a big tip, he suddenly switched to a catchy film tune with a disco beat. The girls quickened their step. Sonalal felt sorry for the confused cobra, who had no idea how to dance to Western music. The whole affair seemed downright vulgar. Then he recalled instances when he too had pandered to foreign tastes, though, of course, not in such a cheap way. Yet the possibility he might have done even worse—for just a few coins—sickened him.

When everyone else had left, Sonalal went up to the charmer, who was still packing up.

The charmer grinned widely. "You liked the show, *sahib*?"

"You're not very good."

The charmer stood up and eyed Sonalal carefully. "You're right, *sahib.* I'm not a great charmer. A man does what a man does. Do you have a problem with that?"

"Have you heard of Sonalal, a charmer at Humayun's Tomb in Delhi?"

"Who hasn't?"

"And?"

"He must be some kind of genius."

A huge smile developed on Sonalal's face. "Then you've heard how well he plays?"

The charmer chuckled. "For all I know, he can't play at all. But who would think of biting a cobra in front of all those foreigners on the day before the Games? What a great ploy!"

"It wasn't a ploy! It was . . . a horrible tragedy!"

"If he'd done it in front of Indians, they would have thought him crazy for trying such a stunt."

Sonalal's face grew hot. "What do you know about charming? Give me that!"

He grabbed the charmer's *been* and began to play. Every note was off-key. It had to be the worst he'd played—ever.

The charmer snatched the *been* back. "You're damn good," he said, wielding the instrument like a club, "but the Lake Palace is *my* territory. Understand?"

Even though Sonalal and Reena dressed and undressed before each other, their intimacy was, oddly enough, almost casual. Sometimes they found themselves sharing the bathroom, he standing over the toilet, she dumping mugs of warm water on her soaped body. Before, she had come to him made up and perfumed—for the sole purpose of satisfying his hunger, palliating the frustrations of his existence. Until then, he'd known her mostly in darkness, through the veil of inebriation. Now he smelled her, not the artificial fragrances meant to hide her own smells. Now he saw all her blemishes, her creases, the puffy flesh on her thighs. Everything was without expectation, without illusion. Reality had replaced fantasy—and was proving itself far better.

With each passing day, Sonalal had become more conscious of an erotic current running through all their interactions. It seemed so easy to take the next step. Restoration of his manhood might not be possible, but then again, in this place it seemed like anything was, and he wanted to try—if only once. But Reena had given no sign her mind had changed, and so he kept his urges to himself.

The bed in their room was perfect. Those first few days, Reena just slept. She slept so deeply, so peacefully, from early evening till late morning, he wondered if she'd discovered a whole different state of being and was reveling in it for fear it wouldn't last. An explosion might occur outside, but he was sure Reena would sleep right through.

Soon the dark shadows under her eyes, residue from catering to vile men in the middle of the night, disappeared. It was as if, after all that sleep, she'd been released from a ghastly burden, eased of a dreadful grief. Happiness seemed to run through her entire body, and sometimes she looked astonishingly like an innocent young girl.

Although he was sometimes guilty of gazing at her sleeping body with the jealous eyes of an insomniac, he also slept well—at least by his standards. Upon awakening, he felt relaxed, as if he'd emerged from a long bath in which the temperature had been perfectly adjusted to his changing moods. Gone was the aching stiffness in his spine, and he was able to sit in positions that only a few days before sent painful shocks into his legs. Oblivious to time, he felt a dozen years younger and almost looked it.

But even under these best of circumstances, he was usually able to sleep no more than six hours. And since they went to bed early, he got up well before dawn. In those few hours of solitude while Reena still slept, he paced outside, listening to the morning yawns of the lake, unencumbered by tensions that snatched away the enchantment of dawn back in Delhi.

With the first red rays of sunlight, he saw the waves on the lake begin to scintillate, separately at first, then gradually together. Birds sang songs he'd never heard in Delhi. They reminded him of birds he used to listen to by a stream outside his village. As a child, he'd hoped one day to know the names of all those birds: yellow birds with greenish wings, red birds speckled with orange, blue birds with purple around their eyes. Now, some forty years later, he couldn't name any. At the moment, his ignorance didn't concern him. The birdsongs were so lovely, it seemed sinful to reduce them to the calls of birds with particular names.

They often took the launch to the main shore. The city was full of palaces, temples, *havelis*. But Reena had no interest in buildings. One afternoon, she asked him to go with her to Pearl Hill, which overlooked Lake Fateh Sagar. The view from the summit was supposed to be one of the finest in Udaipur. Also at the top was a famous statue of Maharana Pratap, the legendary Rajput warrior-king who had refused to surrender to Akbar.

On the way to the bus stop, they passed a roadside *chaatwala*. The man's cart didn't look very clean, but Sonalal was hungry. He downed two plates of *dahi badas* with extra red pepper, three plates of *pani puris*, and a plate of *samosas*, and finished with a mango. Reena said she wasn't too hungry and just chewed a slice of mango.

The mango's smell reminded Sonalal of the ether and also of what Doctor Seth had told him about benzene. He wished to share his insights with Reena—impress her with his knowledge of science. So he held the mango peel before her and said, "It has been shown by learned men that a mango smells like a snake biting its own tail."

Reena gave him a very queer look.

He realized how ridiculous it must sound to her. Without any understanding of science, how could she be expected to appreciate such subtle knowledge? Nevertheless, he was determined to teach her a little science. So later, while they stood in the bus queue, he did his best to explain. "There was once a foreigner named Kuku or Kuloo or something like that. This fellow was trying to understand benzene, which is what makes mangoes smell so wonderful. Then, one day he dreamed of a snake biting its own tail, and he realized that's what benzene was like. And this smell of benzene, amazingly, is also the smell of the ether that connects everything in the universe."

Reena looked perplexed, and it occurred to him that he didn't really understand it either, even though he was absolutely sure it was true. "Anyway," he said with authority, "that's why a mango smells like a snake biting its own tail. It's called science, Reena. From science, they have learned that if you go so fast your skin burns off, time moves backward. Did you know that? And did you also know that our bones are made inside stars?"

She seemed to ponder his words for a moment. Then she asked, "Does that mean that when a snake bites its tail, it gives off the aroma of a mango?"

He didn't think so, though he couldn't explain why.

She was still staring at him, waiting for an answer. Eventually he said, "Reena, it's much more complicated than that."

She didn't seem to like the patronizing tone of his answer and remained silent a while. At last she said, "Look, the bus is coming."

The bus dropped them off some distance from Pearl Hill. It had been an unusually hot week for this time of the year, and when they finally reached the summit, they were covered in sweat. With his back to the statue of Maharana Pratap, Sonalal's eyes took in the view in one continuous sweep. The heat had kept people out of the sun. In the glassy light, the world below seemed pristine, the lake serene, imperturbable. He realized how tired he was of Delhi—growing each year, crowding, spreading, squeezing, suffocating. Laloo had once said, "There are more people in India than in the whole world." Only now did Sonalal understand.

While Reena rested on a rock and absorbed the view, he walked over to the statue of Maharana Pratap. The warrior-king was mounted on his horse, gaze fearless, ready for battle. As Sonalal admired the statue, he imagined Maharana Pratap hiding in the rugged mountains around Udaipur after his defeat by Akbar's army—thirsty, nourishing himself with wild roots, alternately finding solace in the stark beauty of the desert and raging over the loss of his kingdom—ultimately gathering the strength to retake it, hobble Akbar's empire. Such courage! He thought about what Jagat had said about local kings' not mattering next to Akbar. Yet here was a local king who definitely mattered—even after four hundred years, even beside the mighty Akbar. In fact, at that moment, Maharana Pratap seemed to matter more.

Sonalal felt like roaring an ecstatic war cry, something so loud it would echo for centuries. Then he remembered Reena was just a short distance away. If he roared, he'd have to explain. He swallowed his roar.

He walked back over to Reena. She was as he'd left her, contemplating the view. She smiled when he sat beside her. Warm breezes swept toward them from over the lake. Sonalal watched a butterfly hover over a rock, then alight there. The insect didn't move for a long time. He wondered if it had fallen asleep.

A wordless hour went by. The sun crept down to the horizon, and the sky became like colored glass. Working outside all day until sundown in one of the smoggiest cities in the world, Sonalal had witnessed magnificent sunsets, but none like this. His eyes lingered on a distant junction of land, water, and sky. It occurred to him that such a place might be the source of great music, an entrance to heaven.

He admired the profile of Reena's face, beautified by glistening droplets of sweat. Her hand was less than an inch from his. All these years he had never held it, just held it. Now he wanted to. The act seemed simple enough, innocent enough—certainly compared to other things they'd done. And right now, he wanted to hold her hand much more than he'd ever wanted to kiss her, caress her, nibble on her neck, or even make love to her. But he restrained himself. The moment was too valuable to risk. "Love but not *love*," she'd insisted, and now he was worried she might confuse one kind of love with the other. He himself was confused. For the first time since undergoing the changes of adolescence, the two kinds of love had become inextricably mixed up again.

That night, they strolled on the hotel rooftop. The moonlight reflected everywhere—on the surface of the water, on the marble palace walls, on Reena's pupils. When Sonalal saw the moon in her eyes, he dared to think the world was theirs. He'd never felt such love. It took all his power to resist embracing her.

She left to get ready for bed. He remained outside, pacing around, trying to control his passion, which seemed to arise from some source deep within him he thought had been lost forever. For the first time in months, he was hopeful for the future, and this hope fueled his passion all the more. Well past midnight, his urges finally quieted down, and he went back to the room where Reena lay fast asleep.

The next morning was the only time she woke up before him. When he finally opened his eyes, he heard her singing in the bath:

> "From which place did you come?
> And to which shore do you fly?
> Where will you stop to rest?
> And what are you looking for?"

Her voice was splendid. All these years, she'd never sung in front of him. He just lay in bed listening to the thousand currents in her voice. She sounded so happy his eyes filled with tears. He fell back asleep for another hour.

At breakfast, he said, "Reena, you have such a great gift! How come I've never heard you sing before?"

She tightened her lips. "There are a few things—not many—that I have never sold, not even to you."

Her tone made him feel insecure. It sounded remote, final. Was she hinting something more?

"But you will sing again, won't you?" he asked. "For me, I mean—when we get back to Delhi."

She gave him an enigmatic look but said nothing. He didn't push her.

At last he asked, "What was the song?"

"One of Kabir's. His songs were about the only things that could make me happy at those times in my life when all else was despair. And there have been many such times."

"I hope now isn't one of them."

"What do you think?"

He smiled. "It was a wonderful song. Kabir, you say?"

"Do you know the story of Kabir?"

He knew Kabir was a saint, but he couldn't recall specifics. With all the side stories of the great epics, not to mention the endless *Puranas*, he was amazed anybody remembered anything. He shrugged.

"I'll tell you, then."

He didn't want to hear the story. He just wanted to sit quietly with her.

"Kabir was loved by Hindus and Muslims alike. When he left this world for his *samadhi*, his body still remained—covered by a shroud.

His followers argued over what to do with the body. The Hindus wanted to cremate their saint, and the Muslims wanted to bury him. As usual, the two groups were on the verge of blows, when a mighty wind came from nowhere and lifted the shroud off the ground. And do you know what lay under the shroud?"

Sonalal shook his head.

"A bed of the most beautiful and fragrant flowers the world has ever known."

The morning was hot, and the rest of the day promised to be hotter. So much the worse for Sonalal. All the *chaat* and *pani puri* he'd consumed the previous day hadn't been sitting well in his stomach. Shortly after breakfast, his bowels exploded. He ran to the bathroom nine times in two hours. Now he was grateful for the Western-style commode. In his wretched state, sitting was infinitely better than crouching.

Around noon, his diarrhea subsided as abruptly as it had begun. Somehow he'd managed to hide the embarrassing illness from Reena, who'd spent most of the morning outside by the lily pond.

While he watched her nap during the afternoon, he began to think about the legend of Kabir. The story had made a deep impression on him, touched him—especially the part about the flowers the saint left behind.

As he sat there, he thought of how it would thrill Reena to wake up with flowers in her hair. The idea thrilled him too. And so, even though he still wasn't feeling well, he went out to buy some flowers.

He came back a little later with a bouquet of mauve flowers. He'd forgotten to ask what kind they were, but they had a wonderful fragrance. Reena was still asleep, snoring softly. He twisted the stems off two flowers, intending to slip the blossoms into her hair. She was such a deep sleeper he didn't think it would disturb her.

But when he got near Reena, he froze. Suddenly he remembered how Sarita used to ask him to buy flowers for her hair. She'd asked often, over so many years, yet not once had he brought her flowers. And now, standing just a few feet from Reena, he was overcome with shame. His entire life seemed wrong. He set the flowers on the dressing table and left the room.

Outside, he found a spot in the hot afternoon and stood there like an ascetic performing penance. After a while, his head was swimming. His shame grew—boundlessly. For now he was also ashamed about feeling ashamed for being with Reena. Without her love, what did he have? Nothing. Soon his feelings had gotten so confused they became intertwined with the guilt he felt over Raju's death. His punishments—impotence, a shredded tongue, nightmares of Rani's lethal revenge—did not seem enough. So he punished himself even more. He stood outside for hours. Already dehydrated from his illness, his body couldn't withstand the heat. Still he kept standing. His skin became so baked, his throat so parched, his legs so cramped, that the misery in his body eventually equaled the misery in his soul. This was, more or less, the effect he'd sought. He returned to the room on the verge of collapse.

Reena rushed over to him. "Sona, what happened? You look like you're going to die!"

She helped him to the bed. He fell across it, didn't have the strength to straighten himself.

"Sona, you're so hot! I'll call a doctor."

"No. Just some water."

She returned quickly with a glass of water and held it to his lips. He took a few sips. Before he knew it, she'd stripped his clothes off and was applying cool wet towels to his body.

An hour later, he felt more certain he was going to live.

He was ready for questions. But all she said was "The flowers are beautiful, Sona. When you feel better, could you put them in my hair?"

He became aware of the bouquet's sweet aroma, which had filled the room. More than ever, he wanted to put the flowers in her hair. But he still couldn't—wouldn't. He began to feel sick again.

"I brought them for the vase," he said. "It seems so empty."

She looked hurt, and he looked away.

On the night before they were to go back to Delhi, Reena told him many things about herself she'd previously kept hidden. Her father had died of smallpox when she was six. *Sati* was still practiced in her remote village, so her mother jumped into her father's flaming pyre. After that, she was raised by an uncle who molested her from the age of eleven. "So I ran away," she said. "And everyone knows there's only one place you can run to."

Sonalal's expression stayed grim long after she finished.

"Let's go outside," she said.

They wandered on the rooftop, listening to the tender music of the lake. Sonalal was unable to enjoy it, still upset by what Reena had told him and by the realization that tomorrow they'd return to Delhi. Their old lives. He stared at the reflection of heavenly glows on the surface of the lake, trying to capture the image forever. He knew he'd never be back.

When they reentered their room, Reena turned to him and said, "Sona, give me your baby."

At that moment, lovemaking was far from his mind. While she'd been dressing earlier in the day he'd sensed it was that time of the month: Her breasts were pointier, the flesh around her buttocks more taut. Even so, her request, almost an order, was totally unexpected—if for no other reason than the minor matter of his impotence. But Reena's eyes seemed to tell him it was a problem of the past. He almost believed it and became aroused.

"Come to me, Sona," she whispered in a voice that stirred him as never before.

As he embraced her, he felt a few anticipatory drops of stickiness in his groin. And with that—the realization he was a man again—he surged heroically.

But then she said, "This is the last time."

"What do you mean?"

"Tomorrow we'll go back to Delhi. Separately. We won't see each other again."

He was shocked. "Ever?"

"Yes, Sona."

His desire was gone. "But why?"

"Because it can never be like this again, and this is all that I want."

"But—"

"You must promise. Do you?"

She stared at him as though he were taking a solemn vow.

He nodded, barely.

"Say you promise, Sona."

"I promise," he muttered.

She lifted her sari. He gently pulled it back down.

He walked over to the vase that now held the mauve flowers he'd bought in the afternoon. He twisted two flowers off their stems, then came back and placed them in her hair.

"Now," he whispered, "let me hold your hand."

She gave him her hand, and they spoke no more.

When he opened his eyes in the morning, she was already gone.

17

THE FLAT, barren countryside gave way to shantytowns, shanty-towns to city, and then the train screeched to a halt. When Sonalal stepped onto the railway platform in Delhi, his old world began to club him. Noise, stultifying smells, pandemonium. He felt paralyzed as he stood amid a whirlpool of unknown faces. Porters loaded with luggage kept grazing him, cursing him. Second by second, the manhood he'd rediscovered last night seemed to evaporate. But so did everyone else's. He felt like a tiny insect among countless others.

The train whistled, ready to depart. He seriously considered getting back on, headed for nowhere in particular. But he took a moment too long to decide, and by then the train was moving too fast to jump aboard.

While he rode the bus home, he kept thinking about the vow Reena had exacted from him, the firmness in her voice, the sad look in her eyes. Did she really want him to stay away? And forever? The thought scared him now, as it had last night. But now, there were other things to fear.

He stepped off the bus, took the longest path home. The closer he got, the slower his gait became. When at last he saw the light in the lone window of his home, he stopped, shuddered. How would

Sarita react? He knew. What could he do to lessen her fury? Not a thing. He'd just have to take it. All of it.

He opened the door a little, poked his head in. The boys rushed over to hug him.

"I told all my friends you went away on important business," said Ramesh. "Did it go well, Papa?"

While he patted Ramesh on the head, he glanced into the kitchen, where Sarita was stirring a pot. She stared at him, her face expressionless. He tried to appear as contrite as possible.

"Your food will be ready in a few minutes," she said with the greatest calm in the world. "I just need to add some more spices to the *dal*."

Right then, he was certain she planned to poison him. She was much too cool. What was she really adding to the *dal*? Rat poison, maybe. When they lived in the trans-Jamuna slums, there had been a case of a woman who killed her husband by mixing rat poison into his food. The man bled to death. Surely Sarita hadn't forgotten the incident. People don't forget such things. At the right time and place, that kind of idea gathers its own momentum—and then, just like that, a man is dead!

He survived dinner. Even afterward, nothing happened. In the beginning, he couldn't make sense of Sarita's behavior. But over the next few days, it became clear she'd just given up on him. He pitied her. In marriage, things that were never right could never be set right, and now he wished he'd been better to her. What must she be feeling? A woman as proud as she couldn't bear so great an insult. And this was just the worst of many. He'd never done anything to make up for all that humiliation—as if anything could. But he might have tried.

He could have taken her somewhere, maybe to the Taj Mahal. She had once been so eager to view it under the full moon. Agra wasn't all that far, really. And if not the Taj, he could have at least bought her an ice-cold drink on scalding summer afternoons. Maybe he couldn't help being a drunken lecher, but once in a while he might have taken her to see a film and enjoy a *kulfi* after.

During the uneventful week that followed, there were times when it seemed as if mending things a little wasn't altogether impossible— moments when the evening breeze stopped smelling stale, when telephone-wire birds sang like nightingales, when the afterglow of sundown stirred remote memories of what might have once been romance. At these moments, he thought of uttering a few gentle words to erase a little pain. But he held back, unsure of her reaction.

One evening, almost two weeks after he returned from Udaipur— while he and Sarita sat alone finishing a late dinner of rice and *channa-aloo*—there was another such moment. He seized the opportunity.

In a wistful voice, he said, "Sometimes I wish we'd gone to the Taj. It must be so beautiful under the full moon."

"The Taj?" she replied, obviously surprised he should bring up that sore point after all these years. "Just as well we didn't."

"Who knows? Life—our lives—might have been different."

She stared into her almost empty bowl of *dal* as if searching for an answer in the patterns of uneaten lentils. Then she said, "Our lives are what they are."

It became so quiet he could hear two mosquitoes buzzing in different parts of the room.

"Our lives are what *you* made them," she added.

Though he might have raised points of qualification, the essence of her accusation was true enough, and he didn't know how to reply. So he just said, "Then again, I've spent a good part of my life sitting in front of a huge Moghul tomb. And the Taj Mahal is probably not that different from Humayun's Tomb. So why go all that way?"

Sarita's gaze hardened, and he knew he'd made a mistake—violated her dream. He readied for the inevitable.

"How do you know so much about the Taj?" she asked in an offhand way.

"From what people say, nothing else."

She bit her lip. "You talk like you've been there. Have you?"

"Never," he said.

But it was one of those times when the truth sounded like a lie. Sarita began to grind her teeth.

All of a sudden she stood up and hurled the bowl against the wall. "Admit it! You've been there! Maybe with a whore of yours, maybe that one you're so fond of—that Reena! You showed her the Taj under the full moon—didn't you?"

Flabbergasted, he shook his head.

"Oh, don't look so innocent, Sona. I know. I've been listening to your dreams for years. A man who cheats on his wife shouldn't talk in his sleep. For much too long, I've suffered quietly."

"Quietly? Hah!"

"Shut up! I'm sure you went to the Taj. Why did you have to go there, of all places? You chose the Taj just to spite me! I curse your evil whore!"

He couldn't bear to hear Reena insulted, even if it was by his wife.

"Your tongue is so sharp I'm surprised you don't spit blood!" he shouted.

She smiled bitterly. "And, Sona, your brain is so dull I'm surprised you can speak at all."

They glared at each other with two decades of anger.

Life had been rich and beautiful when he was in Udaipur, but now, such a short time later, it seemed horrible, with every indication of remaining so forever. Sonalal fell into a depression he couldn't find his way out of. Food lost its taste, and he ate almost nothing. Whole days went by without his smiling. He moved slowly, like an arthritic old man.

He longed for Reena. In seconds, her smile would soothe his aching soul, and her touch would endow him with the strength to beat back his despair, give his life a future. Without her, it wasn't much use to be a man again. Of course, he was grateful for what she'd done. And it had also led him to wonder if, in time, she might be able to help him find his music—though that miracle was probably too much to hope for. Then again, who knows?

Were it not for his promise, he'd have gone to Reena right away. But he was convinced she wanted him to honor his vow. And yet, he spent much of his energy fighting the impulse to break it. Somehow he managed not to succumb. He was exhausted by the struggle. He needed support to keep standing, to go on. In the end, he took his anguish to Jagat. But though Jagat comforted him with warm words, he couldn't tell Sonalal what he needed to know to snap back to life.

Only one person could.

But when he showed up at Doctor Seth's office, the doctor's assistant smirked and said, "The old fool is in jail."

The ancient gramophone in the drawing room was playing a popular Hindi film song. The tune was supposed to be catchy, though the hollow sound emitted by the crackling machine made the song sound old and sad.

"Why is he in jail?"

The assistant didn't answer, just kept smirking.

"Why?" said Sonalal, his voice suddenly anxious.

"His usual idiocy."

"How's that?"

"A woman came complaining that her husband forced her to do all sorts of things against her wishes, if you get my meaning. Your friend, Doctor Seth, said she should fight back—bite back. For some reason, he'd recently decided biting was the solution for everything. And look at the trouble he's in now!"

"Her husband died?"

"No, but she bit the place all men prize. And her husband is a deputy police inspector."

"After all, Doctor Seth didn't—"

"Serves him right. The quack thinks he's some great genius. For so many years, I've heard him give people the craziest advice: make a pilgrimage somewhere walking backward, brush your teeth with red pepper, eat tomatoes till your fingernails turn red, and lately, this biting nonsense. I put up with it because he paid me well—and because I had big gambling debts. Well, now they're paid up, and just in time too."

Sonalal kept silent while he tried to figure out what to do.

"I'm going to start my own practice," said the assistant in a different tone. "I'm qualified. I nearly completed a bachelor's in psychology. Perhaps you—"

"Which jail?"

"You're not going there, are you?"

"Which jail?"

"The one near Kashmiri Gate."

———————————————

Sonalal tried to persuade the constable at the jail he was Doctor Seth's nephew.

The constable squinted suspiciously. "A nephew isn't close enough. If you were a son, that would be different."

Sonalal pulled out ten rupees from his pocket.

The constable laughed. "Ten rupees won't turn a nephew into a son!"

Twenty did.

"Come along," said the constable. "I'll take you to the old man. Poor fellow doesn't look very good. He'll die here, you know. The deputy inspector isn't a forgiving type. He developed quite a reputation during the Emergency—he probably would have broken the fingers of J.P. himself! And now, word has gotten around about what his wife did to him. I think the deputy inspector will punch the next man who gives him a funny look. And he'll just keep getting your uncle's appearance before the judge postponed."

Sonalal followed the constable down a stinking corridor lined with iron doors. At the very last door, the constable fished into his khaki shorts for a ring of keys. He hummed a film tune as he tried one key after another.

"Ah, there!"

The door creaked open. The tiny cell was bare and dimly lit. Doctor Seth lay on the concrete floor wearing a prisoner's uniform, evidently asleep. The doctor looked very frail, withered. Miserable as Sonalal was, he didn't have the heart to disturb the poor man with his own problems. He was about to turn away when the constable slammed the door behind him.

Doctor Seth opened his eyes. "Who's there?" he said, fumbling for his eyeglasses.

"Me, Sonalal."

"Sonalal?"

"The charmer."

"Oh, Sonalal," said Doctor Seth, as if they were back in his office. "My most interesting patient. What now?"

"Are you sure you want to talk?"

"Of course, of course. Sit down. Not quite as luxurious as my office, but it will have to do."

Sonalal sat cross-legged on the concrete floor.

"Now what is it?" asked Doctor Seth.

Sonalal didn't know where to begin. He took a moment to gather his thoughts, then said, "It's like this. I'm in love with a woman who doesn't want to see me again. My wife hates me. Raju, whom I loved more than my own sons, is gone forever. Once I was the greatest charmer in the world. With a few notes from my *been,* I could bring immense joy to snakes and people; but now I can't please a single creature in the whole world. Nothing has turned out right."

Having blurted it all out, Sonalal felt slightly naked.

"Life can be that way," said Doctor Seth, staring at the wall.

"But I don't understand why it has to be!"

Doctor Seth put his hand on Sonalal's shoulder and said, "One spends most of life trying to understand it in the wrong fashion. Some thirty years ago, I read the entire encyclopedia, A to Z. Then, because I wasn't sure I'd grasped all of it, I read each volume again. The power of my spectacles had to be increased four times while I did all that reading. Years of work—all for nothing. One wastes so much of life, maybe the whole thing."

For a second, Doctor Seth became so pale Sonalal thought the old man was going to die right there. But then the doctor smiled. It was a faint smile, yet there was a hint of the old impishness in his eyes. The color started to return to his face.

"Are you all right?" asked Sonalal.

"I think so. You know what just occurred to me? This. No matter how much effort you put into getting from A to Z, you somehow manage to end up at A all over again. And yet there is something in that. Do you know what I mean?"

"I'm not sure," said Sonalal. "Are you saying it's like a snake biting its own tail?"

"Hmm . . . I'll have to think about that. Anyway, go on."

"Well, what should I do?"

"About which of your many problems?"

"I might be able to live with the others if I could just make great music again."

"That may never happen."

"But why?"

Doctor Seth scratched his earlobe. "In the desert, there is a cactus that grows fifty years before it flowers. And then it flowers only one night—that's it."

This wasn't what Sonalal wanted to hear. "You know what I've been thinking? That maybe I can't play anymore because I smashed my new *been* after Raju died. Do you think the *been* could have been special? Magical?"

"Ah yes, the magic *been* theory. Listen to me, Jack. There are no magic *beens*."

"How can you be so sure?"

"A man makes music. A *been* makes noise."

"You used to be more helpful."

Doctor Seth stood up with difficulty and began walking around in circles within the narrow confines of the cell. "All right," he said. "Unlike medical doctors, I haven't missed a diagnosis yet. And those charlatans don't cure, just palliate. That way you keep going back, and they keep getting richer. But I've always had a cure rate higher than a hundred percent. Now is not the time to falter. So let's try to re-construct how all this happened. As I recall, you played beautiful music. The cobra was exhausted but, because of greed, you forced it to dance, even though the snake was like your own son."

"Maybe it was greed," said Sonalal, "but I just wanted to make a little extra money so I could try a special liquor, that's all. But then both Raju and I got so carried away by my music, neither one of us was thinking. You see, the music was so beautiful—"

"Yes, yes, whatever. Anyway, then you bit the snake. It bit you back."

"No! The other way around! Raju bit me first."

"Who bit whom is not the issue, am I right?"

"I suppose not."

"Now where were we?" said Doctor Seth, stroking the white bristles on his chin. "Oh, yes—the bite. You became famous for biting the cobra, but you wish it were for your music. Now you are no longer famous, not because of anything to do with your music, but because people have forgotten the biting. And somehow because of everything, you can't even play a cheap film tune. Is this correct?"

"More or less."

"Frankly then, I see no reason why you shouldn't be able to play beautiful music again. The music came first, and nothing that happened afterward should affect your ability to play. So, go now, make great music. Go, go, and be done with it!"

"It's not so easy. Can't you just tell me what to do? The tongue-biting trick worked very well."

Doctor Seth shook his head gravely. "Biting has become a very dangerous treatment."

"Then tell me something else."

Doctor Seth's eyes developed a remote look, and he didn't speak for some time. At last he said, "All right then, I'll tell you something else. In the old days, just after Independence, I went all around India by train. I'd been something of a Congresswala, and I felt it was important to know my country. There were less people then, and India was a better place. While traveling through the South, I was amazed by all the marvelous temples and statues. On the coast bordering the Arabian Sea—far off the beaten path—I came across a very unusual place. It was full of large statues, mostly of people, but there were no temples. Even more strange, no one knew who built the statues or why. And yet they were so magnificent against the setting sun! Yes, those were some of the most moving moments of my life, standing before those lonely statues while waves crashed against the shore and the figures became shadows against the red sky. Those statues are beautiful every evening at sunset. And they will always be beautiful. Always—today, tomorrow, and long after you and I are gone—even if no one ever sees them again. All my life I've puzzled over what those statues mean. Now I know. They don't mean anything. They are just there. It doesn't matter who built them or why."

"I don't understand what all this has to do with me."

"It has to do with beauty, and that is what you seek, isn't it?"

"I just want to create—"

"Then you have to risk it all, maybe even your own life. Why do you think so many women die in childbirth?"

Sonalal frowned. As usual, Doctor Seth seemed to be going out of his way to be obscure and difficult.

"But what about science?" asked Sonalal.

"Science tells you the exact temperature of the sun. How will that help you live your life?"

"You once told me it had all the answers."

"Did I? Well, that was then. I'm wiser now. And I can tell you very clearly that science is science, life is life, and that's that."

"But—"

"Listen to me. Once there was a man called Schopenhauer, who said life is suffering, nothing else. He was right. But even so, there's something in suffering that is unique, yours, and yours alone. All your pain, your guilt, your grief, is yours, only yours. It is one of the few prizes life gives everyone."

The old man was making no sense at all to Sonalal. "Please!" he said. "Can't you just tell me something specific to do—like eating tomatoes till my fingernails turn red?"

"No."

"Why?"

"Tomatoes only work for the anemia of loneliness."

In the middle of the night, Sonalal suddenly woke up gasping for breath. His heart was racing, his hands trembling, his face all sweaty. He had dreamed he was an albino cobra with pearly-white scales and pinkish eyes. He was so rare, so coveted, collectors from around the world were willing to pay lakhs for him. Every snake catcher in India was after him.

Sonalal got out of his cot and paced around the room, unable to make sense of his dream. Of course, Doctor Seth would know what it meant; Doctor Seth knew just about everything. But what a peculiar man! The doctor could easily have helped him this morning—if only he'd wanted to. Instead, the old man had played dumb, going on about strange statues, cactus flowers, pregnant women, and whatnot. Doctor Seth had to be hiding something. And how could the doctor be so sure the smashed new *been* wasn't magical? How? No question, Doctor Seth was harboring some secret critical for getting his music back. The villain! No wonder he was in jail!

Daylight's arrival didn't diminish Sonalal's suspicion. If anything, it became stronger. He was absolutely convinced his entire life hung on a secret only Doctor Seth knew, a treatment only Doctor Seth could prescribe.

So, without washing his face or even drinking his morning tea, Sonalal rushed out to catch a bus that would drop him off near the jail. Even if the treatment Doctor Seth ordered was horrible—even if it meant brushing his teeth with hot pepper and then biting his tongue every night for a year—he'd do it. Starting tonight.

A different constable was on duty at the jail. This one was an older man with a wild grin, who looked like he'd be much more expensive than twenty rupees.

"I've come for Doctor Seth," said Sonalal.

"He's not here," replied the constable in a surly voice.

"What?"

"I said he's not here!"

"Yes, I heard what you said. I meant, where is he?"

"Now, that's an interesting question."

"And?"

"Who are you anyway?"

"His nephew—but more like a son."

The constable's expression suddenly changed. "Oh, I'm sorry, then."

"Why? What happened?"

"Your uncle . . ." The constable hesitated.

"Yes?"

"The old man made such a racket yesterday evening! He was raving—barking all sorts of crackpot nonsense. And he kept begging us to give him a tomato. A tomato! What did the old man want with a tomato? Nobody could figure out what was wrong. Anyway, he eventually quieted down. And then, around three at night, they went to check on him. He was dead."

18

S ARITA MAY have given up on Sonalal, but she still had to live with him. And Sonalal had nothing to do. At home much of the day, he clashed with her over the most trivial matters: who should refill the pot of drinking water, where he left his clothes, how long she spent in the bathroom, who snored louder, whether her family had given his family suitable gifts at the time of their marriage. In all those quarrels there were plenty of openings for her to bring up more substantive issues, but Sarita didn't lose her self-control. Freed from the threat of further escalation, Sonalal became even more contentious.

At dinner one evening, Sarita brought him some *puris* she'd fried only minutes before. He lifted the top *puri,* which was still quite warm but no longer hot, and grumbled, "They're all cold!"

Her face became askew from anger. For a second, he feared anything could happen. But she quickly regained a modicum of composure. A long silence followed, during which he scarcely breathed. Then Sarita issued a command: "You will find a new cobra tomorrow."

He looked away. "I don't think I can ever charm again."

"Listen, Sona. You are a charmer, only a charmer. When I hear you go around moping about immortality and the meaning of life like some great *rishi*, I want to laugh. What do you know about such things?"

He felt the wound and prepared for the sprinkling of salt: to hear for the ten-thousandth time what an illiterate fool he was.

But her tone suddenly became gentle. "Sona, not so long ago you were the best charmer in Delhi, maybe even all India. The best! For all I know, you still are. So few people are lucky enough to do what they are best at; God constructed the world so most never even find out what they are best at. But God has not just given you a gift, Sona. He made sure you were born into a family whose only profession is to utilize that gift. And lest you still be confused about your purpose, God made you totally useless at everything else."

In all the years he'd lived with her, she had never acknowledged his talent, and right then, it meant more than any fame he could imagine. If she, of all people, said so, then he really must have been the best. Once.

"I've lost it. Without Raju, I'm no good."

She shook her head. "If you keep at it, if you wait long enough— who knows?—you might be great again."

"You cannot step into the same river twice," he said.

"So people say. But isn't the Ganges eternal? The same with other holy rivers. And if they're all eternal—unchanging—then why can't you step into the same river twice?"

That got him thinking.

"Sona, if you just sit around pouting, nothing will happen, and besides, we'll be paupers in no time. You must charm again. You must!"

There was logic in her words. In a world without Raju and Reena—in a world with only Sarita—all he had was charming. It was his only purpose in life. And what if Sarita was right? Maybe it really was possible to step into the same river twice! If anyone could, he could. For his was a great talent—so great even Sarita was forced to admit it. Suddenly he feared that, by not charming all this time, he'd offended the gods who'd bestowed such an extraordinary gift upon him, and that was why he'd been unable to play a decent series of notes on his *been*. The gods were punishing him!

"You're right," he said with the urgency of the recently converted. "I must charm! There's nothing else."

She seemed amazed he agreed so readily.

Even he was amazed. And he was more amazed at the sudden surge in his affection for Sarita. For now he realized seventeen years together meant something, something terribly important. He wanted to hold her, kiss her, and—for the first time in many months—make love to her.

He stepped forward. She stepped back.

And yet her expression still showed a hint of warmth. He took another step toward her. This time she didn't move away.

———————————————

The next day, he scouted all around Delhi for a cobra. Somewhere in the huge city there had to be a snake who could measure up to Raju. Sonalal knew where to look. By late afternoon, he had examined nearly three dozen cobras offered for sale by snake catchers from all over India. Kashmiri snakes, Punjabi snakes, Orissan snakes, Bihari snakes, many more. But none seemed to have even a tenth of Raju's talent. He wasn't even sure if they could hear.

With charming in his immediate plans again, at the end of the day he made his way toward Humayun's Tomb. He wanted to let everyone know he'd be back soon. To charm. As the great red edifice came into view, he imagined the excitement his announcement would bring—the cheers, the applause. Suddenly his legs became heavy, and he felt sharp shooting pains in his chest. His gait slowed, then came to a halt. He couldn't go into the tomb again without a cobra. Tomorrow, he'd head off to the countryside and catch his own. That was the only way, the way he'd found Raju.

And so, only a few hundred meters from the tomb, Sonalal turned around. The sun had just set, but he wasn't ready to go home yet. Although last night had been surprisingly gratifying, he knew nothing had really changed between Sarita and him; it was best to enter the house only after she had fallen asleep. So he headed for Connaught Circle, as good a place as any to pass time.

Today it seemed a particularly long walk, and once there, he kept walking—following the flow of people making their way around the huge circular shopping mall. Over the years, he'd made many such circles of the mall, but this evening it bothered him: circling, circling, more circling. He had to go somewhere else—stop circling. He exited onto a side street.

Eventually he found himself at Jantar Mantar, the medieval astronomical observatory built by the Rajputs. He wandered some, then sat down to rest. It was quiet, no one around. Surrounded by sundials and the massive triangular structures of the observatory, he gazed up at the evening sky. He was in a mood suited to stargazing, and he stared at sparkles in the smoggy heavens for a long time. Could his bones really have been made in those stars? The more he thought about it, the sillier it seemed. For that matter, so did that business about time going backward. And did it make any sense for a mango to smell like a snake biting its own tail? If it hadn't come directly from Doctor Seth's mouth, he'd have dismissed it there and then. But the dead doctor had been right about so many things.

Sonalal recognized a few stars, among them Trishanku. As a boy, he used to believe Trishanku was his own special star. Tonight the star seemed to emit some fantastic glow, bestowing a little calm, a little courage. He squinted at other stars, attempting to peer into depths of the universe. But the moon, almost full, was very bright and conspired with the smog to limit his view. He recalled how his sons often argued over whether the Americans had gone to the moon. Like Ramesh, Sonalal had never quite believed in the moonwalk. And now, as he viewed the moon, it seemed terribly important to know whether a man had really walked on it.

Yet even as he wished with all his heart that a man had set foot upon that huge silver ball in the sky, he feared it was a hoax.

He whispered to himself, "You just have to decide."

But he couldn't.

$\mathcal{E}$ARLY THE next morning while it was still dark, he caught the first bus to the Interstate Bus Terminal on the other side of Delhi. There he boarded another bus to the hills where he'd grown up. It had been years since he'd been back. Once it had been a place to escape from, but now it seemed a good place to return.

After two hours on the bus, the countryside began to look familiar. Back in the city, he'd always remembered the terrain to be far more luxuriant—green trees everywhere, fields thick with wheat, the soil wet and dungy. Although it had recently rained some, the yellowish color of the fields brought back memories of drought and the way things had really been.

The bus dropped him off so close to his ancestral village he decided to go there first—just for a look. The morning was filled with light pleasant breezes, and long ribbons of clouds stretched across the sky. As he walked along the dirt path to his village, he passed field after field with buffalo teams plowing the land, working water wheels.

Soon he was at his village, a world of brown earthen dwellings, bullock carts, wandering goats, clay pots, old men smoking hookahs, women kneading dough. All said, the place hadn't changed much. But the people had. He even recognized a few, now many years older than when he'd last seen them. Although there were some curious glances, no one recognized him. Or if they did, they didn't care to renew the acquaintance. He considered searching for his cousins, debated. In the end, he decided there wasn't much point. He'd become an outsider; this past was lost. Though the thought saddened him, he also felt unburdened of the thousand rules and restrictions of village life.

For a while, he watched several boys in frayed shorts play *kabadi* in the village *maidan*. In his youth, he'd earned a certain fame for his skill at the game, and he contemplated showing the boys a trick or two. His own cricket-crazy sons weren't interested in *kabadi*. He was about to say something to the boys when he noticed a stray dog. It was uncanny how much the creature resembled a dog he used to have, part village mongrel and part wild. As a boy he'd been quite shy, and the dog had once been his closest companion. He used to talk to her, and she'd listen with ears pricked up, sometimes nodding as if in comprehension. But when the next drought hit and threatened to turn into a famine, his father didn't let him feed much to the dog. As rats became scarce, the skeleton of a dog began to lap up scum floating on stagnant ponds around the village. Then, one evening, the sickly beast vanished—probably died scavenging the countryside. Sonalal remembered crying for days.

It was time to go find a new snake. Sonalal took one sweeping look at the place where he'd been born, where six generations of his family had lived and died. Would he ever come back? Would any of his descendants ever see this place?

He turned around and walked away. For the next two hours, he trekked through a hilly area just beyond the village. It crossed his mind that, if still alive, Rani might be lurking somewhere in these hills. But it felt so exciting to be back in his youthful haunts, so rejuvenating, his mind quickly moved on to other things. Occasionally he stopped to listen to orchestras of chirping birds, leaves rustling in the wind. But mostly, he was taken by the quiet. He'd forgotten how quiet it could get—how beautiful that was. He felt far from everything, free. He climbed up and down hills, sucking in fresh air. He realized how sick he was of the dreary, dusty flatness of Delhi.

It had been nearly fifteen years since he had caught a cobra. He'd learned how from his father, a legendary snake catcher said to possess a sixth sense for snakes. While he scanned the terrain, the rules his father taught him came back quickly. Because of the recent rains, the chances of nabbing a cobra were good. "When wet, search high and dry," his father used to say. Since his father would find a snake almost everywhere he looked, Sonalal began his search among the highest, driest rocks around. It felt good to hunt, use his hands; he had turned into something of a *sahib* these past months.

He'd brought along a bamboo pole with a metal spike for rock turning and defense, a set of bamboo tongs, and a thick-walled cow dung container capped by a lid weighted with stones. So equipped, Sonalal began to turn over rocks. He had first spied Raju under rocks such as these—maybe even one of these very rocks. Young Raju was as agile and wily a snake as he'd ever seen. Raju kept dodging every attempt to capture him—seemed to make a game of it, hissing in a way that was more like a human snicker than an animal sound. It was only after Sonalal finally trapped Raju that he heard his new cobra growl—and what a fierce growl it was! Even his father marveled at the feisty cobra he'd brought home that day. It took many months to train Raju, who didn't submit to any of the standard maneuvers. Only when

Sonalal began to treat Raju with affection did the snake show any inclination to dance.

Sonalal kept flipping over suspicious rocks. Underneath them he found many snakes, mostly harmless country types. But no cobras. Just when he was about to take a break, he turned over a large dry rock and saw the first cobra—a female guarding her hatching nest. Most of the eggs had small openings with tiny black noses poking out. He'd seen similar sights before, but they hadn't moved him as now. It was like witnessing a miracle. He sat at a distance he believed wouldn't threaten the mother and watched as the brightly colored baby cobras broke out of their eggs. It made him think of when Sarita had been expecting Ramesh—of how he used to place his hand on her swollen belly so he could feel Ramesh's gentle kicks. And sometimes at night when it was very quiet, he'd gently press his ear against her belly and think he heard faint heartbeats. Back then, he'd been so excited about having a family.

As the tiny snakes struggled to free themselves from their shells, it crossed Sonalal's mind that some of these cute hatchlings would eventually grow into magnificent cobras. He wanted to take one back home. Raju could never be replaced, but maybe if he started with a baby snake, loved him like a son, raised him in an atmosphere of great music, and taught him to dance, then who knows? Sonalal was almost ready to nab a hatchling when it occurred to him that it would be quite some time before one of these snakes was old enough to charm—and he couldn't wait.

At last the baby snakes began to crawl off into a world of snakeskin purses. Only then did Sonalal realize the afternoon had arrived, and he hadn't caught a cobra yet. He got up and moved on, turning over rocks along the way.

Soon he came to a clearing on the hillside. At first, he didn't recognize the spot. There were many new trees, and some old ones had disappeared. Then he saw *his* tree. As a child, he used to sit on branches of this very tree for hours—daydreaming. In his teens, he'd come here to think, escape from a village where every day was like every other.

He spotted what had once been his favorite branch—the most distorted of all. Now, it reminded him of a snake's tongue; there was even a place where the branch forked into two new ones. The branch point was thick, smoothly curved. That was where he used to sit, nestling his buttocks in, dangling his legs. When the tree was full of leaves, he used to be virtually hidden up there. At one time or another, he'd spied everyone in the village from his hideaway. Once he even saw his father come there with the potter's wife and have sex with her right under the tree, no more than ten feet from his eyes. At the time, he'd thought them both old—though they were no older than he was now—and he found the sight disgusting.

He tried hard to remember his father. He couldn't remember him the way he believed a father ought to be remembered. He recalled what his father had looked like, what people used to say about him. He recalled a man who had taught him how to turn over suspicious rocks without being struck by the snake beneath and a dozen other tricks, although now it seemed that he'd learned all the important things about charming on his own. But he didn't remember much else about the man he'd lived with every day for over twenty years.

He realized he'd never really known his father, and the thought filled him with sadness. But also, in a strange way, with relief. All his life, there had been a hole inside him, and though the hole would never go away, now he knew where it was.

Again he looked at the tree, his favorite branch, the branch point where he used to sit. How would his old perch feel after all these years? He had to know. His legs had lost their spring, and it took more than a few jumps. Finally he was up there. He scanned the jungle from his new vantage point, spotted a peacock scampering through the brush. He tried to imagine what it would be like living in this tree as a hermit, existing on berries and roots.

The reverie didn't last long. His buttocks were a little bigger now, the fit no longer precise. And his genitals, droopier than they used to be, kept getting in the way. He squirmed but couldn't rid himself of the kind of discomfort only a man can know. He jumped off clumsily, fell to the ground. He rose slowly, then shook the lower half of his body to rearrange what had been displaced by the tree. He gazed at the old tree one last time. Then he turned around and resumed his quest for Raju's replacement.

Under the very next stone he flipped over was a cobra, again a female, but quite old. She rose on end, hissing, her hood spread. There was a quaver in her raspy hiss, and she was straining to maintain an attack position. From his nightmares, Sonalal quickly recognized her. And if he had any doubts, they vanished when he noticed the markings on her hood—exactly as he'd dreamed.

She was Raju's mate: Rani.

Even without the bamboo stick in his hand, he knew he could

have won any struggle. But he was overwhelmed by the rage in Rani's eyes. All his guilt came back—the guilt not only from having made Rani a widow, but also from effectively making one of Sarita. His mouth flooded with bitterness. He dropped his snake-catching gear and knelt before her.

Rani hissed and growled with new fury but didn't seem ready to lunge. She just stared at him. Fear invaded Sonalal, and he thought of begging for mercy. He decided he didn't deserve any. What murderer, adulterer, and worthless father deserved mercy? He had no saving grace—except possibly his music. But a few beautiful notes remembered by no one couldn't absolve him for being the foul man he was. Besides, maybe his music hadn't been so great, after all. Maybe he'd deluded himself all along into thinking he'd moved the gods. Where were these heavenly tears he was so sure about? Could it all have just been in his head? Anyway, now it didn't matter. Rani's venom would spread throughout his body, killing all that was rotten in him. It was the kind of perfect justice only the gods could have planned. Who was he to question what had been inscribed in the patterns of stars long before there was any Sonalal, Raju, or Rani?

"Kill me quickly," he said in a choked voice as he stared into Rani's angry eyes. "And don't taste my blood for long. I'm poisonous too."

Rani hissed again. Sonalal prepared for her fangs to pierce his flesh, wondering where she'd strike first and how painful death would be. He closed his eyes, waited. After a few seconds, he had no idea where Rani was, for she'd stopped hissing. There was no sound anywhere. At first, the absolute silence shook his insides; never had he been so aware of his beating heart. But the impossibility of escape eventually brought a certain calmness to him. He allowed himself a final thought, and it was of Reena.

When at last he opened his eyes, Rani was still on end. She'd moved closer and was within easy striking range. At this distance, in this position, he couldn't defend himself. And yet, when he peered into Rani's eyes, he didn't feel afraid anymore. Her anger was gone, and all he saw was layer upon layer of sadness. Her eyes seemed to hold the pain of all living things. After a while, he could no longer meet her gaze. He couldn't bear all that sadness.

He waited for Rani to decide what to do. Finally, she lowered herself and slithered away, ever so slowly.

Sonalal remained kneeling, wishing Rani had struck.

He wept a long time. When at last he stopped, he was drained, dazed. With dusk less than an hour away he considered going back to Delhi without a snake. Then he thought of Sarita's reaction. Either he went home with a snake or he didn't go home at all.

He sighed, took some deep breaths, and resumed his search, venturing into the densest part of the jungle. In no time he was finding snakes everywhere. Once in a while, he so startled a snake that it curled up and rolled down the slope like a ball.

Some of the snakes he found were cobras. But either they squeaked like mice or growled like tigers. None had the right temperament. Snakes, like people, had different dispositions, and the cobra Sonalal was searching for had a personality complementing his own. It wouldn't be love, as it had been with Raju—simply companionship, an arranged marriage based on a brief assessment of suitability.

Just as he overturned a particularly promising rock, up sprang a cobra, hood spread, its scales shining in the sunlight. Right away, Sonalal knew this was the one. The snake was about four feet long and swayed from side to side with adolescent bravado. Sonalal carefully closed in. Then his foot slipped on a small rock. He managed to keep his balance, but the bamboo tongs in his hand fell to the ground, just inches from the snake's tail. If he picked them up now, he'd almost certainly lose the cobra. Worse, he might get bitten and die right there, his body consumed by ants.

He decided to use his hands. While circling the cobra, he snapped the fingers of his left hand, then made a shrill whistle. When he thought the snake looked confused, he feinted, and his right hand shot in to grab the creature's neck. The cobra wriggled wildly, lashed him with its tail, nearly got free. Sonalal tried several times to pin the snake's tail down with his foot while avoiding a bite by the other end. Each time his foot missed. Finally his sole landed square on the cobra's tail and held it against the ground. The snake seemed to sigh, as if he understood the battle was lost. Then he suddenly began to squirm with new energy. For another two minutes, man and beast struggled, before Sonalal was at last able to thrust the enraged creature into the cow dung container and slam the weighted lid on it.

Sonalal plopped onto the ground, breathing hard. For half an hour, he held the cover down as he listened to the cobra thrashing around in the container. Eventually the snake quieted. Sonalal was a little disappointed that his new snake had given up so easily. With Raju it had taken much longer.

By the time Sonalal made it to the roadside with his new cobra, the moon and stars were out. He worried he had missed the last bus of the day. While waiting, he listened to a growing band of crickets. The chirping soon became a continuous blare. How did such tiny creatures make so deafening a racket?

After nearly an hour and no sign of a bus, Sonalal became resigned to sleeping by the road until the first bus arrived in the morning. Then he saw headlights approaching. A minute later, he and his new cobra were on the bus back to Delhi.

Sarita and the children were asleep when he got home. He tiptoed around until he found a piece of rope. Then he tied down the lid of the cow dung container so the cobra couldn't escape if the container somehow tipped over. He debated whether to bring the container into the house or leave it outside. Ultimately he decided leaving the snake outside would be a bad start to their relationship. As it was, friendship was hard enough. And who knew what the poor cobra was already thinking—kidnapped, far from home, in a flat dusty place with no trees?

So Sonalal left the container just inside the door. Then he lay down on the floor next to the thick-walled vessel, so he'd be the first one bitten in case the cobra escaped despite his precautions. Sonalal was so tired he fell asleep in minutes.

Just before dawn broke, Sonalal had a dream. He dreamed that Raju had descended from a place beyond the highest clouds. Raju's expression was as tranquil as the Buddha's, and he moved with a grace that surpassed anything of this world. Sonalal tried to talk to Raju, but there was no reply. Raju just looked at him and smiled faintly. After some time had passed, Raju began to sway back and forth, as if to some melody. But Sonalal heard nothing. As the call from another world grew stronger, Raju slowly floated up and then dissolved into the clouds.

When he opened his eyes, Sonalal didn't know quite what to make of his dream. But it was the least upsetting dream he'd had in a long time, leading him eventually to conclude that it must be some kind of omen—otherworldly support for his new beginning. And so, later that morning, he defanged his new cobra and extracted its venom glands. He spent the next few days getting to know the snake, helping him adjust to city life. Sonalal understood how hard that could be, for even he hadn't fully adjusted after all these years. But the cobra proved more adaptable, and within a few weeks Sonalal began to train him. Though the new cobra didn't have anything close to Raju's talent, he was intelligent, with a good sense of balance, and quickly learned how to follow the *been*. Sonalal congratulated himself on a wise choice.

Sooner than he'd anticipated, Sonalal was back at Humayun's Tomb, wearing his mauve turban, waiting for tourist buses to rumble in, coughing amid their black exhaust. Once again, he was hopping on buses, playing his *been* while he traipsed up and down the aisle, then jumping off and charming his new cobra before crowds of tourists.

Those first days were hard. His heart just wasn't in charming. He kept thinking about Raju, and tears would sometimes roll down his cheeks in the middle of a show as he charmed his new snake. And yet the pressure to turn in a high-quality performance turned out to be much less than he'd expected. Though his fingers felt clumsy—as if wrapped in thick bandages—no one appeared to be listening to his humdrum music. No one even seemed to remember what had happened only a few months before.

In a short time, Sonalal's eyes reddened from dust kicked up by people and vehicles, his skin cracked and itched during a new dry spell, his hands developed the blisters of a working man, and it felt as good and bad as the old days. It was just as well his new cobra didn't have Raju's ear. For although Sonalal was eventually able to play a lively tune, it wasn't anything like the past. To avoid getting too upset over the quality of his music, he kept telling himself it would take time. But while he required the patience of the afternoon sky, he was impatient as ever. He thought he'd go mad living the rest of his life like this. His only peace was in diversion. Soon he was drinking and whoring with a vengeance, as though it were his last chance to rediscover youth in the vapors of alcohol and the warmth of women's bodies.

20

SUMMER LEFT, then came again, and again—and just like that, seven years went by.

Sonalal's hair had thinned, and his once flat belly had grown. When he was naked, his paunch—big enough to partly obscure the view of his shrinking genitals—looked unsuited to his limbs, now skinnier than ever. His gums were gradually ejecting the three loose teeth still in his mouth. Age had spurred the growth of his prostate gland, and he had a tendency to dribble all over the bathroom floor, much to Sarita's annoyance.

Sonalal's cobra, now well into middle age, had turned out more or less as expected. Although the snake could be moody, he had become a skillful dancer. And yet, after several thousand shows, Sonalal couldn't remember a single truly inspired performance of the sort Raju used to deliver three or four times a day, day after day. He was never quite sure how much this cobra really cared for music, and sometimes he wondered if the snake could hear at all. He was now convinced Raju had been endowed with a special talent for appreciating music no other snake ever had. A divine gift. And this eventually led Sonalal to conclude that it was Raju's genius which had allowed him to create such magnificent music. But even if Sonalal wasn't what he used to be, he was sure that, if he wanted, he could still play as well as any charmer in Delhi—though he was more aware than ever of the huge distance between that conventional excellence and the kind of music that made the gods cry.

With time, Sarita had accumulated significant savings. Sonalal now realized that much of the money the foreign journalists had given him—the four or five thousand Sarita once claimed not to have—had been placed in an interest-bearing bank account in her name. And over the years, she'd been adding to it—partly from the large portion of his income she always held on to, partly from what she earned doing needlework. So now they owned a radio, a tiny gas stove, and, just this summer, a small electric fan that buzzed like a hive of angry bees. The spot where the fan was to be aimed had led to a major family squabble, and the fan was now aimed at no one and thus stirred no air worth stirring. But Sarita and the boys often contemplated the electric fan as though it was a prize, evidence the family would never slip back into poverty again.

Yet money didn't mean much to Sonalal. Seven years does a lot to the way a man sees the world, and he'd finally come to that point in life where his greatest satisfaction was some peace of mind and three hours of restful sleep. That may have had a little to do with why he no longer frequented brothels. But the main reason was impotence. It was physiological this time—owing to sugar in his blood, the doctor said.

His impotence wasn't complete, though, which had initially made it all the more frustrating. After a string of embarrassments over his erratic tumescence, foreplay had turned into sheer terror. Even when it produced the desired effect, he still had to get through the sexual act. And his worries about the rest of his performance usually guaranteed failure. He'd even failed with older, more patient prostitutes, including the same ones he'd once recommended to Ratan the Great—though these days, the blind magician's libido had improved so much he slept only with young women, often two at a time. For, as Ratan the Great himself had predicted, he had grown much younger. And when he looked straight into the sun, he claimed to see flashes of light. This had generated a lot of excitement among fellow magicians, who hoped Ratan the Great would soon see well enough to perform the rope trick.

Although Sonalal no longer went to brothels, he still went out drinking. And drink he did. Since he usually got home well after midnight, he rarely ate with Sarita and mostly slept in the hall. The little conversation that took place between them had become so cautious it was almost meaningless, burdened as it was by a history of bickering over countless nothings.

Sarita did what she could to redeem him. In recent years, she had become religious. Every morning, she filled his mouth with *prasad* and sacred water after she returned from the temple. He seemed to have a permanent vermilion mark on his forehead, so often had she done his *teeka*. All this did little to change his ways. But he was glad she derived deep satisfaction from her belief. It seemed to compensate, at least in part, for the life he'd given her. She now ascribed everything to inscrutable divine will, which somehow put her sad world in perspective, erasing much of its painfulness, he being a notable unerasable exception.

He felt no small remorse. He realized that he cared about her and, in some peculiar way, loved her. For he'd come to the conclusion that love was the capacity to tolerate each other's bad smells. Seven years ago he'd thought he couldn't bear her odors anymore, but now he had finally gotten used to them again. Occasionally, he believed it was just his impotence that made her look good these days—sometimes even in that particular way—but he knew there was more to it. He respected her devotion to the boys, her cleverness, her fierce will— even if it continued to often be directed at him. Maybe she wouldn't build a tomb for him upon his death as Haji Begum had done for Emperor Humayun, but she was still the woman who'd sit beside his burning funeral pyre, and that meant something—something important. Even so, he wished Reena could be there too and hoped news of his death would reach her in time.

Although he'd thought of Reena every day during those years, he kept his vow. There had been times when he desperately wished to see her, but as much as breaking his promise, he feared disturbing the memory of their week together in Udaipur. He often thought of Lake Pichola, glimmering under the sun, forever rippling, never ruffled. When life became too trying, that week of love, along with those few notes he'd played for the gods the night he bit Raju, seemed enough to get through it all. If he died tomorrow, if he turned into smoke the day after, it wouldn't have been all for nothing—at least that was how he sometimes saw it.

21

*I*N SEVEN years, Sonalal's sons had changed too. Even though Sonalal still had his doubts, both Ramesh and Neel now agreed the Americans had reached the moon. Considering their father's looks and physique, they'd turned into surprisingly strong, handsome boys; Sonalal noticed that neighborhood girls passed by the house much more often than before.

The boys were doing fairly well at school and, more than ever, embarrassed by their father's livelihood. Like everyone else, they had forgotten the day he was the most famous man in India. Once he'd been proud of his sons, their learning, their similarities to the sons of schoolteachers and bank clerks. But now the time had come to initiate them into the family tradition. He wanted them to charm—be charmers. He wished to pass his art on to the next generation. If his sons had any talent whatsoever, he'd turn them into the best charmers in all Delhi.

The trouble was that the boys didn't see charming in their future. For years, Sarita had been telling them there was nothing like a government job. "A government clerk never gets fired," she often said. "And businessmen pay them lots of money just to move a file from one desk to another."

And so the boys dreamed of working for the government, though Ramesh, the more ambitious of the two, had his sights on a position beyond the merely clerical.

One evening, Ramesh said something at dinner about wanting to go to college; Sonalal had kept quiet before Ramesh, but later he turned to Sarita and said, "You've raised the boys' expectations much too high. We may have come a long way from the village, but it's a lot longer to get where you want them to go."

"It may be long," she replied, "but it's not impossible. The boys are already better educated than many members of Parliament."

Sonalal had never seen it like that, and the thought momentarily filled him with pride.

Then Sarita added, "It really bothers you that your sons are so much more capable than you, doesn't it?"

"No."

"Then what do you really want?"

He dared not say. He didn't want to get her going, for his handicap was already very great. Ramesh and Neel had always been their mother's boys. Now they were old enough to decide for themselves what kind of father he'd been—and Sonalal knew their judgment was getting harsher by the day. He could scarcely even talk to the boys. And Ramesh, at times, was openly defiant. How would he ever turn his sons into charmers?

_____

On a Saturday morning when Sarita was at the temple, Sonalal and the boys happened to be drinking tea together. At what he thought was the most opportune moment, Sonalal said, "There's no occupation as noble as charming."

His sons exchanged amused looks.

"There is no need for charming in modern India," Neel finally said.

"Except to amuse foreigners," added Ramesh. "As if we haven't amused them enough these past two hundred years!"

Both boys chuckled.

That made Sonalal furious. "Charming is a great profession!" he shouted. "For seven generations, *our* people have been charmers. With music we have made snakes do what only gods can make them do. And how? Because we play not for foreigners or even cobras, but for the heavens."

Sonalal then smiled mysteriously, as though a divine audience gathered every time he played. "I can teach you all that," he said. "Do you remember what Saigal could do with his voice? Well, maybe you are too young. But I can teach you how to do that with a *been*. Even more! After all, Saigal couldn't make a snake dance, could he? And the gods listen to my *been* with the same attention you listen to cricket test scores on All India Radio. Tell me, what person who works for the government can command the attention of the gods?"

"They can command people," said Ramesh. "And they can send their children to college. Can you do that?"

Sonalal glanced away and said in a weak voice, "One day, you'll understand how hard it is to be both a father and an artist."

"But you are neither," said Ramesh.

Sonalal felt like wet cow dung.

Neel gave his elder brother a sharp look. "You shouldn't have said that!"

Ramesh bit his lip and stared at the ground.

Everyone was silent. After a few minutes, Sonalal got up and slowly walked to the other room. It was one of the many times in life he wished for a daughter. How he'd love his baby girl, kiss her, pamper her! And he would become a good man for his daughter—good inside, good outside. He'd protect her from the world of men. Men like him—and much worse. But as he contemplated the evil in the world, he thought maybe it was better not to have a daughter. For if he wasn't a good man—frankly, he wasn't sure he could be—she'd judge him harshly. She would suffer. And then he too would suffer, much more than he'd ever suffered. He was sure he could bear just about any suffering—except his daughter's.

Although disappointed in his sons, Sonalal wasn't about to give up. He *was* their father. A weak one, a negligent one, perhaps no better than his own father had been to him—and maybe even worse, as Ramesh seemed to think—but a father nonetheless. And they were his sons, his blood, his only blood. His line! He wanted them to do what he wanted them to do. A father's right. If he had a doubt or two about urging his sons to become street performers when they might lead more prosperous lives, those doubts quickly succumbed to his belief in the sacrifices required for great art. Even so, at times he wondered if he'd have been as persistent had his own talent remained intact. With the young, at least one could hope. Besides, it wasn't as if he was pointing the boys in some useless direction. What could be more worthwhile than genuine art?

And so, with unusual stubbornness, Sonalal began to work on Ramesh; he exerted more subtle pressure on Neel only because the boy was less rebellious and didn't shave yet. But first he had to establish proper respect in the minds of his skeptical scions. Why should his sons want to be charmers if they, like Sarita, believed their father was an illiterate fool? That was the real problem. So, at every opportunity, he tried to impress his sons with his knowledge of the world.

One such opportunity arose on an evening Ramesh and a classmate were studying together: Sonalal overheard Ramesh say "benzene."

He hadn't heard that word in years. Could it be the same benzene? He had to find out. Half an hour later, when Ramesh's classmate left, Sonalal sneaked up behind his son, who was hunched over his textbook. He waited quietly until Ramesh finally sat up straight. But then Sonalal saw it—the same circular shape Doctor Seth had once drawn.

"What are you studying?" Sonalal asked.

Scarcely glancing up from his book, Ramesh replied, "Science."

In his school uniform Ramesh still seemed boyish, but his voice was almost a man's, and there was more than a touch of arrogance in it.

"Benzene?"

Ramesh couldn't have appeared more surprised. "You've heard about benzene, Papa?"

Sonalal nodded. "I used to know a lot about science," he said, trying to recall what Doctor Seth had told him years ago. "Unfortunately, I've forgotten most of it. But don't you think benzene looks like a snake biting its own tail?"

Ramesh seemed truly dazzled by his father's insight. "I never thought of it like that. You're right, Papa. The chemical structure of benzene really does look like a snake biting its tail!"

Sonalal patted his son on the shoulder. "Ramesh *beta,* when you get older, you'll be surprised how many things look that way."

In a short time, Sonalal had said all he possibly could to convince his sons that charmers were as smart as anyone who worked for the government. Unfortunately, the corners of his factual knowledge were round, and soon he was having to make things up. To his chagrin, his sons were catching his fabrications. The boys simply knew too much. Even about such an innocuous topic as the weather, they were full of answers. They knew why the sound of thunder occurs so long after a flash of lightning, why a rainbow has so many colors, why the Monsoon always starts in the South, scores of other facts that robbed the world of its poetry. Rather than risk further damage to his credibility, Sonalal changed tactics.

"I have to admit," he told the boys, "just after Independence, it was really something to work in the government. I remember when *sarkari* officers rode into our village on horses, and it was as if maharajas had come to visit. But it's different now. These days they can't even get matinee tickets for a film!"

And at least once a day, he mentioned illustrious men who'd followed the paths of their ancestors. He reminded the boys that Asoka was the grandson of Chandragupta, that Maharana Pratap was the son of Udai Singh, that Sanjay Gandhi was the grandson of Nehru. And, of course, there were the Moghuls: Shah Jahan, son of Jahangir, grandson of Akbar, great-grandson of Humayun, great-great-grandson of Babur. Sometimes Sonalal even included Aurangzeb in this succession of Moghul fathers and sons, which he recited musically. As much as he wanted to, he refrained from mentioning Sonalal, son of Chandilal, grandson of Pannalal, great-grandson of Motilal, great-great-grandson of Heeralal—for fear of overdoing it.

In this way—with a craftiness his sons would never have suspected their father capable of—he continued to attack on multiple fronts: making fun of the government and the westernized people who ran it, extolling tradition and things uniquely Indian. He had no idea what the boys were thinking, but every now and then they seemed to be listening.

On a cool January evening, he asked the boys, "What if Shah Jahan hadn't followed in his father's footsteps? Tell me, what then?"

Ramesh and Neel shrugged almost simultaneously.

"There would have been no Taj Mahal—that's what!"

"You have a point," said Ramesh.

Neel nodded in agreement.

That gave Sonalal a little hope his blood was finally asserting itself. Of course, ultimately it had to. For it was strong blood, warm with talent, every bit a match for Sarita's cold carping blood, which until now had ruled Ramesh and Neel.

The boys still had thoughtful expressions on their faces; they seemed to be mulling over the matter. Sonalal realized this was the chance he'd been waiting for. He seized it.

"The whole netherworld trembles before the greatest charmers," he said, in a way that made it sound like he kept the fiercest demons at bay with music from his *been*.

The boys looked intrigued.

So Sonalal cracked his knuckles and launched into a discourse on the special powers of great charmers, the importance of artistic professions. By now his arguments had gotten quite polished, and as he made his impassioned speech, he was more convinced of its truth than ever. At last he was ready to conclude: "Your father is the best charmer in India. And you are the only two people who share his— my!—blood. Which means you can be great charmers too. For the power to charm comes from the blood. It is a sin to take this gift lightly. Anyone can stamp papers for the government, but how many can entertain the gods with the music from their *beens*? As far as I know, there are only three such people in the world, and they are in this room. And remember this. A man can either be a cauliflower or he can attempt great things. There is nothing in between."

But that evening happened to be one of the few times when Sarita was actually paying attention to Sonalal's utterances.

"Have you no shame?" she roared. "You lie to your own sons! Leave my children alone! Stop trying to brainwash them. Thank God they don't want to charm for a living. Don't you dare try to change that. Don't make them like yourself! You don't really care about them. You just want to live through them, now that your own skill has dwindled. Oh, how I've suffered so this wouldn't happen! Stuck in poverty, married to a drunkard who prefers suffocating his family with *beedi* smoke to saying a few kind words, an illiterate oaf who thinks being befuddled his whole life makes him a philosopher, a man who has satisfied every woman in Delhi except his own wife . . ."

Sonalal thought of pointing out that at least he didn't gamble. But Sarita's eyes were bloodshot—burning with some insane wrath—so he kept quiet.

She continued her diatribe, rattling off all his transgressions—railing like an Opposition leader, speaking faster than a cricket commentator. Pale from rage, she pounded her closed fist on the table while she characterized every detail of her suffering that came to mind—until he too felt its horrible weight.

He didn't know if everything she said was factually correct; he couldn't remember that far back. But if even half of it was true, that was too much. He felt immense pity, and his face flushed from shame.

She found it impossible to stop. She kept spewing and gushing the past, listing his numerous sins. On and on, she went—words, words, more words—until she'd run out of new things to say and was repeating herself.

But by then, he was back to pitying himself, not her.

She looked exhausted. As her tirade wound down, she said, "Do you think I'm such a miserable wretch, such a spiteful shrew, for no reason at all?"

He took the question to be rhetorical. But she stared at him as if she expected an answer, putting all her monumental bulk into her gaze. He was angry enough to say yes. After a struggle, he mumbled the word incomprehensibly.

"What?"

"Yes!"

She covered her face with her hands, then began to cry. She almost never cried. She was too proud an adversary. Yet now she couldn't stop. She groaned and howled like a mortally wounded animal. He couldn't help but be moved. After she'd cried for ten minutes, he sat down beside her. He ran his finger gently over the purple veins on her temples, kissed her wet eyes. He wanted to say something meaningful, but there was really nothing to say. So he put his arm around her and listened to another half hour of sobs so violent they made him shake.

His sons had witnessed everything. And from their faces, it was clear whose side they were on. As he sat there with his arm around Sarita, Sonalal realized the power to charm that was in his blood would end with him.

22

*F*OR NEARLY a year, Jagat had been appearing consumptive—a sallow complexion, black rings around the eyes, sunken cheeks. He looked like a starving man. Dr. Basu had taken him to the best tuberculosis specialist in Delhi, but the disease was detected too late for a man Jagat's age. Soon he was coughing up blood.

On a morning early in February, Jagat told Sonalal, "A man can leave this world gently or not. Do you think it means something, Sona? Better to fall into a pit of vipers than go like this."

Jagat coughed until tears filled his eyes, then spat more blood onto an already bloody handkerchief. He smiled faintly and added, "But I'm the only man in the world who'd have the misfortune of surviving a pit of vipers."

He died sometime that night, the coldest of the winter.

Dr. Basu was the only other friend of Jagat's present at the cremation. As he and Sonalal stood by the pyre waiting for the priest to begin, the doctor whispered, "It pains me to know so few came to bid farewell to a man who saved so many."

Sonalal tightened his lips but said nothing.

"After Jagat died," the doctor went on, "I was planning to drain all his blood. There was enough antivenom in Jagat to treat every poisonous snakebite in the country for months. But as usual the damn phone was down, and I heard about it too late. When I finally saw Jagat, his blood had already clotted."

Sonalal stared disbelievingly at the doctor.

"Don't look at me like that," said Dr. Basu. "It was Jagat's idea. As his closest friend, you'll know this is exactly the kind of thing he'd have wanted. It's a shame I missed the chance. One dead man could have saved thousands of lives. That's the kind of miracle only great *rishis* can accomplish."

Sonalal nodded grimly.

The priest instructed Sonalal to light the pyre, then began to mutter, "God is Absolute Truth, to utter the name of God is Absolute Truth. . . ."

The flames rose high.

"Stand back!" said Dr. Basu. "Your *kurta* will catch fire."

Sonalal was baking in the heat, but he didn't move. Those flames were terribly important, and he wanted to experience them as fully as possible—burn a little too. He'd brought along the urn containing Raju's ashes, which he'd saved all these years, and when the fire was at its peak, spitting and coughing as Jagat once had, he tossed the ashes into the flames.

With Jagat gone, Humayun's Tomb really felt like a tomb. Laloo was the only one left whom Sonalal considered a friend, their old differences long forgotten. All the liquor Laloo had swallowed over the years had finally affected the magician's brain and turned him into a surprisingly pleasant fellow. No matter how rotten the weather was, Laloo began every conversation with "What a marvelous day it is!" And then he'd smile in an almost saintly manner, as if he could at last smell the ether that flows through the universe. But Sonalal missed the old cantankerous Laloo. This Laloo had almost no memory, and memory was just about all Sonalal had.

Sonalal smoked incessantly. The pile of *beedi* butts left near his spot at the end of the day was a much-discussed topic at the tomb. He'd begun to cough up thick yellow-green sputum. Initially, the ugly stuff came only in the morning, but soon he was spitting it out just about anytime. He knew it was due to all the smoking, though he didn't slow down. He needed his *beedis*. So he smoked and coughed, and coughed and smoked, and people joked that he was the main source of exhaust in Delhi.

One warm afternoon in late spring, when there were almost no tourist buses and nobody to talk to, Sonalal began to dwell on old dreams. He felt like he'd compromised on nearly all he cared for—and lost all. On only one thing he'd refused to compromise: his music. Hadn't he given everything for it? Yes, everything. He'd tried his utmost, paid in sincere tears and even blood, yet all told, it hadn't amounted to much. But if he had failed, maybe there was some nobility in his failure, although not nearly as much as he'd hoped. Not enough to redeem. He had once hoped his love for Reena might somehow make up for much that had gone wrong in his life, even at the cost of adding to his family's scorn. And yet, what had come of that love? Those days in Udaipur, the happiest week of his life, had led to nothing but wistfulness. What might it have been? If only he and Reena had found a little courage, everything might have turned out differently.

The pull of the past was too great. He had to find Reena. He hadn't seen her since that last night in Udaipur. As far as he was concerned, he'd honored his vow. For much too long.

As soon as he stepped off the bus in front of the Red Fort, Sonalal's heart raced and palpitated. Chandni Chowk had changed more in seven years than in the previous hundred, yet he navigated the narrow streets like the local postman, inhaling the pungent odors of humanity, energized by the din of the bazaar.

On the way, he came upon a crowd gathered around a man selling some kind of medicine. "Boons and blessings in a bottle," said the man, eyes sparkling with sincerity. "These pills contain a long-forgotten ancient remedy." He went on to say the pills prevented birth deformities, cured cholera, guaranteed a full moon on the night of your eldest daughter's wedding. The pills were also efficacious for standard ailments like rheumatism and gout. "And most important," said the man, "the medicine slows down the process of aging. In America, which is a very advanced country, they sell snake oil for this purpose. Of course, what I have here is at least as potent as snake oil and is especially suited for the Indian constitution. . . ."

The man raised the pill bottles and gazed up at the sky as if to tempt the heavens. "For only ten rupees—"

"Ten rupees is too much!" someone yelled.

The seller wasn't offended. "Yes, ten rupees is not cheap. But you must understand, the price of these pills changes. Twenty years ago, they went for thirty-five rupees a bottle, and thirty-five rupees was a lot then. Later, when people lost faith, the price dropped—as low as two rupees when the prime minister was assassinated. However, recently people have become disillusioned by science and other foreign scams. They are going back to old ways that made India great before the foreigners almost destroyed us. With demand so high, I'm afraid I can't negotiate on the price. And think of it like this. For ten rupees, you'll live ten years longer. Is one rupee a year really so expensive?"

Sonalal elbowed his way through the crowd and bought a bottle.

When he came within sight of the brothel, he automatically glanced up at Reena's balcony. This afternoon he didn't see her petticoats hanging. Instead, two monkeys sat on the railing, grooming each other. He guessed Reena had shifted to a different room. Just as well. Her previous room was cramped and next to the toilet. He recalled being woken at odd times by the sound of flushing.

He went up to the old wooden doors, knocked. A crow cackled somewhere. He knocked again, hoping Reena herself would answer. While he waited, he found it impossible to keep romantic film scenes out of his head. He tried to imagine how Reena would look: plumper, with fine permanent lines on her forehead, her hairstyle more suited to a woman in her forties. Her hair would have grayed by now, though she'd probably be getting it dyed.

He wasn't exactly sure what he'd say. He had always spoken his mind to her, and maybe it was best to do so now, just tell her that he'd thought of her every day for all those years, that he still loved her. Maybe they could find a way to . . .

The doors creaked open. Before him stood a young woman, almost a girl, seventeen at most. She was very pretty, with a round chocolate face, deep dark eyes. She had silver rings on every finger. She didn't need to be made up as she was. It caused her to look too much like a whore.

Behind her, he could see the old parrot cage. But Raj and Nargis had been replaced by two chirping birds that weren't parrots. He wondered how long parrots lived.

"Yes?" said the girl.

"I want to see Reena."

The girl's face tensed. "Reena is no longer here."

Sonalal's heart sank—and kept sinking. "But where has she gone?"

The girl looked down. Her hands fidgeted with the end of her sari. "To another world."

"No!"

The girl was silent.

His whole body became numb. He concentrated on maintaining his balance. He didn't want to think.

Finally, in an almost inaudible voice, he asked, "How?"

The question was too much for the girl. Her eyes became moist, and her lips seemed to struggle for words.

At last she spoke. "A strange illness. Another sister died too. The illness went on a long time. The doctor said something terrible had gotten into their blood. No one who gets it is spared. And it doesn't kill you just like that. Like *kesari dal*, it eats you bit by bit. Now the doctor comes every six months to check our blood. We're all scared."

Sonalal leaned against the wall for support. His throat felt dry as a desert rock, his eyes as if someone had thrown spices in them. He could hear the blood pounding his temples. The girl was staring at his face. He shut his eyes, listened to a pathetic wheezing sound in his chest that became louder and louder.

After a minute, he opened his eyes. He gave the girl a tormented look and pointed to his wet *dhoti*. With great difficulty, he managed to whisper, "May I come in? You must find me a new cloth."

Grief stricken, he wandered aimlessly through the maze of Chandni Chowk. He plunged into depths of sorrow he couldn't find his way out of. He'd forgotten how much he loved Reena and tried to recollect memories scattered over twenty years. He had always believed one of those memories would be his final thought before he too left the world, and now he sought to ensure this by etching each memory into his brain. But even while he recalled as many details as he could—the smell of her bosom, the softness of her wavy hair, the taste of her neck, the sponginess of her buttocks, the serenity of her voice—Reena receded. She became an apparition, an *asura*—a diaphanous nymph. He realized she'd always played that role for him, and it saddened him all the more that she would remain vaporous forever.

He didn't go home, couldn't. Reena had stayed nearly all her life among these winding streets that again smelled of the blood spilled by Nadir Shah three centuries ago, and he too wanted to remain here. In the vain hope another kind of spirit might soothe his own, he emptied bottles of liquor in single gulps. He staggered from tavern to tavern, including places he knew better than to frequent—where men had gone blind, and liquor was sometimes paid for in blood. He didn't care. At one of those places, he passed out on the floor.

When he opened his eyes in the morning, his head was so heavy he scarcely knew what he was doing. He plodded here, there—nowhere. Around noon, he found himself standing in front of a spice shop. Set out on display were open burlap bags filled with herbs and spices of almost every color. At the very front were piles of tamarinds, intertwined turmeric roots, malformed clubs of garlic, all sorts of peppers. Sonalal's eyes focused on a huge pile of sun-dried red chile peppers. He felt like hurting himself in some way. Suicide by pepper ingestion crossed his mind.

"You want to buy some chile peppers?" asked the shopkeeper, a graying man with a beaklike nose.

"How much?"

"Fifteen rupees a kilo. They're the hottest peppers of the season. I dare you to try one."

Sonalal picked up a pepper, put it in his mouth. His tongue burned. He chewed the whole thing, swallowed. Then he grabbed a handful of peppers and stuffed them all into his mouth.

"I said one!" shouted the shopkeeper. "One! Are you going to buy or not?"

Sonalal's whole face was on fire. His eyes flooded with tears. His nose dripped. His ears seemed about to burst. The top of his scalp felt like it was going to peel off. He stared up at the midday sun until he saw nothing but whiteness.

"You're mad!" screamed the shopkeeper.

Sonalal looked in the direction of the voice but still saw only whiteness. His flaming tongue went into painful spasm. He tried to speak, couldn't.

"Get out of here!" yelled the shopkeeper, pushing him into the street.

He was carried off by the flow of people. As he walked with the crowd, his blindness gradually went away. But his vision remained obscured by a yellow-brown haze that wouldn't lift. All the buildings seemed slanted, off-balance, as if a single shove could cause the entire old city to collapse. His other senses were off too. Everything smelled filthy. He wanted to throw up, but it wouldn't come. So he just walked on, slowly, his feet wandering of their own accord.

Eight kilometers later, night fell. While searching for a place to sleep, he stumbled over two half-naked lovers on the lawns outside the Red Fort. The young man and woman picked up their clothes and ran away.

"Please stay!" he shouted after them.

That only made them run faster. He wept over his crime.

He went back into the dark miasma of Chandni Chowk. For hours, he took random lefts and rights until he found himself in the seediest part of the city, home to addicts, perverts, thugs, whoremongers, pimps, hashish smugglers, assorted other scoundrels. Weighed down by fatigue and sorrow, he slept among footpath dwellers and *fakirs*.

No one beat him, but in the morning all his money was gone. At first, he barely reacted to his sudden return to poverty. It felt right in some strange way. He went without food and paid no attention to how he looked. But eventually he couldn't tolerate hunger any longer. He tried to hawk the bottle of pills that slowed the aging process.

"Live ten years longer for just ten rupees!" he told people in the street, waving the bottle in his hand.

Half an hour later, he was offering a hundred years for a rupee.

But nobody wanted to live longer that day. No one even gave it a second thought. In anger, he hurled the pill bottle against a medieval stone wall and savored the music of shattering glass. Rather than go home, he began to beg.

Skilled in the art of coaxing coins out of people, he impressed local beggars with his style and persistence. But his efforts had little ultimate effect on those with jingling pockets. A few even barked insults at him. In two days, he barely collected two rupees.

"That's quite good," he was told by a boy with no legs who'd collected even less.

He gave all his money to the boy.

For the rest of the day, he roamed through the old city, doing his best to keep his mind off food. It wasn't easy. Starvation had made his sense of smell particularly acute, and it happened to be that time of year when the city was full of mangoes. Their fragrance combined with routine bazaar stenches to create a marvelous odor. He didn't have the strength to resist. So he found a spot not far from a mountain of rotting mango peels, then sat down and inhaled an aroma that could only have been the scent of immortality—the ether.

After a while, he didn't know if the aroma was really out there or in his head, which was spinning pleasurably. High above the three-story buildings that lined the narrow street, he watched twirling kites that children were flying from rooftops. They were spinning, and so was he: Soon the kites started to look like dancing snakes. But as his vision became clearer, he realized the snakes weren't dancing at all. Could it be? Yes—they were biting their tails!

Five hours later it was dark. But now he could finally see. The moon was out, but not so bright that a man couldn't try to understand it—or walk on it. He was sure now: A man had walked on the moon. And suddenly he was sure of many other things too, as unconnected incidents in his life began to form an arabesque at once overwhelming and satisfying to behold. And even though he still couldn't forgive a universe that let a man kill his own son and meted out such wicked punishments to people as good as Reena and Jagat, his grief had become more discrete, crystallizing into a precious gem he'd forever hide from all others.

While loitering on his third day of hunger, in a roadside barber's mirror Sonalal noticed the sad, furrowed face of an old man. It looked no different from a million other faces of haggard old men, and a second passed before he realized that grimy unshaved chin was his own. He ran his fingers through his matted hair, wondered about lice. It was time to go home.

Though he hounded everyone who passed, it still took three hours to beg for his bus fare.

Sonalal got off the bus, slowly made his way home. He coughed amid the reddish-gray dust suspended in the air, the result of construction almost everywhere in the locality. With Delhi bursting with people and land prices skyrocketing, plots in this very modest neighborhood had become worth much more than the old houses that stood on them. And so the landscape was changing fast. Companies were buying up the land, knocking down the old houses, and erecting multistory buildings in their place. Even his landlord, the retired army captain, now in his seventies, was talking about selling the house and returning to his native Calcutta. "The air in Delhi has become as bad as Calcutta," his landlord had recently said. "But at least Calcutta is Calcutta."

If his landlord sold the house, the family would obviously have to move. Where would they go? Sonalal hadn't discussed the matter with Sarita yet, mainly because discussions with her could go anywhere these days.

When he stepped inside the house, familiar sights and sounds lifted his spirits. Ramesh and Neel were arguing over something he didn't understand, and Sarita was washing dishes. Sonalal saw the place in a new light—the single constant in his life, his only safe haven.

Home.

But when Sarita noticed him, she became so furious over his lengthy absence that she didn't take the time to make sense of his unkempt state. "Back to seeing your favorite whore?" she shouted. "Did you go to the Taj again?"

For the first time in his life, he was on the verge of striking a woman.

Sarita's gaze remained full of defiance, and this only fed his rage. But then he saw that the boys were watching, which reminded him of how he'd witnessed his own father beating his mother. He shut his eyes, took a deep breath and a step back, then turned away.

Later, he thanked God for giving him the sense to go outside and puff *beedis* till his nostrils burned. He didn't speak to Sarita for more than a week, and even then, it seemed all too soon.

23

JAGAT'S LOSS had been like an amputation, but for months after learning of Reena's death, Sonalal felt like he himself had died. He had known this feeling once before when he lost Raju, and he wasn't sure he could survive it again. He longed for different times. He feared he couldn't keep up with a world changing so fast, where nothing surprised and anything was possible, even a man walking on the moon.

So conscious was he that death was stalking him, he paid a lawyer to draw up a will. The lawyer said his assets weren't enough to worry about, and since everything was already in Sarita's hands, it was only a formality. But that was exactly what Sonalal wanted: a formal document that told Sarita he trusted her to do what was best for the boys. After so many years, it was all he could offer, and yet it seemed terribly important—an affirmation that, in spite of it all, something had been created in the family, something worth preserving.

But he couldn't bear the thought of Ramesh and Neel seeing their father's thumbprint on the will, reminding them of his illiteracy. So, at the age of fifty-one, he hired a professional letter writer to teach him how to sign his name. His new skill made him feel more intelligent—not because he was now able to write his name, but because he finally realized the ability to write had nothing to do with intelligence. Even so, he signed the brief document with considerable pride. But as he walked away from the lawyer's office, he had the eerie feeling that his blood had turned into blue ink, his bones into paper.

He was developing cataracts, which further darkened his view of a world with too many people and too few trees. Doctor Seth had once told him about the Big Bang that created the universe and the Big Crunch that would end it all. Some nights, Sonalal went to bed thinking the Crunch was imminent. There seemed no point in having any illusions, so he had gotten rid of most. And yet, even on the grayest of gray days, he managed to find solace. Without searching, or even quite knowing what he'd found, he had discovered the satisfactions of a life unsatisfactorily lived. And even though he was no longer able to indulge as before, he still gave it his utmost. A few glasses of liquor added that crucial third dimension to memories of a woman's body. And he was thankful for those memories and many others.

All that liquor didn't make it any easier to get up in the morning. For he was still a poor sleeper, and his bones no longer glided easily under his flesh. He didn't really want to be young again, though he wouldn't have minded a few more years of middle age. Every day he scolded himself for throwing away those pills that slowed down the aging process.

"What's the secret?" he once asked the increasingly youthful, sightful, and lustful Ratan the Great.

"After you penetrate Maya's veil," said the magician, "the universe has no secrets." Then Ratan the Great launched into a speech that became vaguer and vaguer, more and more slippery, until it defied comprehension.

Since his family was no longer desperate for money, and because his heart wasn't in it anymore, he started allowing a young charmer much of the business at the tomb, although he still took a few buses late in the day. The young charmer, who spoke to him respectfully and called him *Chachaji,* was from a village not far from where Sonalal had grown up. Sonalal taught him all he could: how to fashion a *been* and tune it, how to feed and care for a cobra so it performed well day after day, how to vary the music to make the most of a snake's mood, how to keep an audience's attention when the snake was slow to perform, how to coax extra coins out of foreign tourists, other things. Though the young charmer was short on talent, he had a lot of drive. And in time, he was able to play a tune even Sonalal could tolerate hearing twenty times a day.

On the kind of afternoon before the Monsoon that can make life seem like a boring dream, Sonalal sat waiting for the next tourist bus. Earlier in the day, Ratan the Great had announced he was almost ready to publicly perform the rope trick. But the heat soon turned everyone's excitement into skepticism, and even some of the magicians made snide comments.

A bus hadn't come in a long time. Flies were crawling all over Sonalal. He was used to flies on summer afternoons, but right now he felt every one of their feet creeping between tiny streams of sweat on his skin. The city smelled like a clogged latrine. No wonder there were so many flies! And where exactly had their sticky feet been?

It was so hot he could scarcely breathe, and when he did, the air scraped his parched throat. He considered treating himself to an ice-cold cola. But though he could easily have afforded the cola, it seemed an unjustifiable luxury. Lately he'd been scolding his sons for their extravagant tastes—they were pestering Sarita to buy them a new shirt every other month—and here he wanted to sip colas!

He hesitated, debated.

The cold-water man passed by, advertising his divinely cooled water, reminding Sonalal of poor Laloo, who now had eyes yellow as a banana peel and skin covered with purplish marks like spiders—all from the liquor, they said. But Sonalal's thoughts quickly switched to the cold water itself. For the first time, he wondered if it really was cooled by divine tears.

He was just about to go after the cold-water man when he heard a backfiring noise. A bus approached, surrounded by a cloud of dust and exhaust. It was one of those battered tin boxes without air conditioning—the sort only middle-class Indians and foreigners with lost souls tolerated on afternoons like this—not worth the trouble for the two or three rupees he was likely to earn. Then again, if he charmed this bus, he could justify buying himself that cola.

So when the bus stopped, Sonalal got on, intending to give a quick performance, then get his cola and call it a day. He lazily sauntered up and down the aisle, playing a straightforward tune on his *been*, the wicker basket containing his cobra swinging from his shoulder. Then, just as he'd done thousands of times before, he hopped off the bus, set the basket on the ground, and started to charm while tourists crowded around.

Even before the cobra rose, sweat was pouring down Sonalal's forehead, stinging his eyes. The sun burned his face, and his head was starting to swim. He felt tired—and more desperate than ever for that cola. As he performed, he sensed the bones of his joints rubbing unhappily against each other. He'd never quit in the middle of a performance, but the end of this one seemed an eternity away. Maybe the time to retire had finally come. Yes, he decided, this was it, his last performance, the end of a dynasty of charmers. But if this was going to be his last performance, he had to finish—or faint trying. He played on.

Perhaps because of the empty retired existence he envisioned ahead—a life of constant bickering with Sarita until one of them, most likely he, died—his music sounded like a dirge. He tried to get his mind off the dismal future, and his gaze wandered beyond his dancing snake, beyond the crowd, even beyond the tomb. He watched a flock of birds fly high above in triangular formation. The birds seemed to carry his thoughts away as they disappeared from view.

Though he was playing a simple tune—one he'd learned nearly half a century ago and had performed countless times—he suddenly hit a string of false notes.

He didn't even notice the mistake.

Then someone in the crowd shouted, "Watch out!"

He stopped playing and looked around, confused. Only once before had he heard such an intense silence in the midst of so many people. But because of his parched state, it took him a second longer than it should have to realize what the silence meant. As soon as he understood, he felt the cobra's jaws grab his right calf.

The crowd gasped.

Without thinking, as if it were the most natural of reflexes, he bent down and grasped the snake by its head and tail, then stretched it out. He trembled with rage. If a man ever had venom in his jaws, it was this man. His eyes bulged and his mouth opened wide, revealing three rotten teeth set in decayed gums.

A man in the audience shouted, "Are you crazy?"

The outstretched cobra squirming in his hands, Sonalal cried, "I'm going to—!"

He couldn't finish the sentence. His mind was in a whirl. Unable to move, he felt like he was in some kind of limbo, stuck there, trapped for eternity. He did his best to regain control of his whirling mind. Gradually it seemed to slow down. But the cobra was getting heavier and heavier; Sonalal's shoulders were aching terribly. He tried to think. He couldn't believe what was happening—what he was doing. Had he suffered everything just to go through it all over again?

"Put the poor snake down, idiot!" said the man. "The creature has no venom in it."

Then someone else said, "Years ago, a charmer at this place bit a cobra and became very famous. Now every son of a donkey imitates him. Leave the snake alone, you toothless old fool!"

Sonalal would rather have jumped from the top of Qutab Minar than look at all those ridiculing faces. But look he did, frozen in that awkward snakebiting position. And during those seconds—what felt like an entire epoch—he heard every snicker, every cackle, every quip.

The noise grew so loud it seemed like the whole universe was laughing at him, object of some cosmic joke.

At last Sonalal set the cobra down. The crowd, still chuckling, began to disperse while the terrified snake scurried back in the direction of its basket.

"Forgive a toothless old fool," he told the snake in a tremulous voice.

It did not seem enough. Sonalal turned his gaze to the sky, for he had a vague impulse to plead for divine mercy. Then it occurred to him that he was really after something else—a sign it wasn't only his life that had been so fated. But the sky was so blue and unblemished, so immense and unreal, there seemed no way to communicate with it. The sky seemed part of a perfection that could never be known by a man. And yet, he, Sonalal, had once known it. On a day that suddenly felt like yesterday, he had caught a faint whiff of the ether that flows through the universe. Still staring at the sky, he thought the ether must be blue, and way high up there, it smelled like a freshly cut mango.

ACKNOWLEDGMENTS

For invaluable advice and support, I would like to express my gratitude to Doris Cooper, Neeti Madan, David Davidar, Marc Aronson, the Corporation of Yaddo, and, most of all, Birupie and Potto. The lines attributed to Kabir are loosely based on the Tagore translation.

THE SNAKE
CHARMER

Sanjay Nigam

Perfect Moments and
Other Tragedies of Modern Life
An Introduction to *The Snake Charmer*

The Snake Charmer begins with a perfect moment. Sonalal, a middle-aged snake charmer from Delhi, is plying his trade for a group of tourists. Raju, his prized snake, is performing beautifully, responding attentively to the music Sonalal plays on his *been*. It is as if the snake, the music, and Sonalal are—along with the reader—all bewitched, and, for a few minutes, Sonalal experiences the joy that comes when our inner and outer worlds become one.

For most of us, moments like this are few and far between. What is tragic about Sonalal's experience is that his attempt to prolong his euphoria results in its utter desecration when he destroys the very thing that has made his happiness possible. Raju, exhausted, wants to stop dancing. Sonalal urges him to continue. But when the snake charmer hits a false note, the snake rebels, biting his master. In a fit of rage, Sonalal bites Raju in two. The moment is over and the results of Sonalal's attack are disastrous. Sonalal's quest to recapture his perfect moment, and his regret over its destruction, will consume the rest of his life.

With lucid and lyrical prose, Nigam effortlessly weaves humor, realism, metaphor, and cultural commentary, luring the reader into Sonalal's voyage of self-discovery and his quest for the ineffable. Beneath the smooth-sailing surface of the novel, the writer is tackling some very big philosophical and cultural issues. The power of the novel in part derives from the reader's sense that the story is both universal and particular to a time and place. Modern-day India is a country of clashing cultures, a place where disparate forces coalesce and factionalize the population. Nowhere in India is that clash of cultures more apparent than in Delhi, with its chaotic blend of ancient temples and new construction projects, its fly-by-night businesses and generations-old practices, its brothels and teahouses and open-air markets, its oppressive heat and seemingly eternal monsoons.

Although Nigam makes reference to some of the political and social factors that characterize contemporary Delhi—including the accidental death of Sanjay Gandhi, the government's attempts to sterilize adult males, the increase in economic and class mobility, and clashes between Hindus and Muslims—it is in Sonalal's family life that we witness the profound changes taking place in India today. Like many members of his caste, Sonalal is poor and unschooled, carving out a life in a crowded, disordered city. But unlike the generations of snake charmers before him, Sonalal has a chance to overcome his poverty. His sons will be educated and able to achieve careers and knowledge beyond what Sonalal could ever have hoped for. His wife's dreams of prosperity are, just barely, within reach. Sonalal's passion, snake charming, is perceived by most of the population, including his family, as a shtick performed solely for the busloads of foreign and native tourists that visit the city. Nevertheless, he is content to live his life working at his ancestral trade, secure in the knowledge that he is the world's most talented practitioner of a dying art form. Standing at the crossroads, where the old and new India converge, Sonalal is confused, misunderstood, and searching for ways to satisfy his many desires.

It is this very search, motivated by the deepest sorrow and a yearning for redemption, that moves us to sympathize and empathize with this frail and slightly comical man, who, though hardly of Ulysses-like stature, is nonetheless caught up in an odyssey of mythical proportions—so fundamental are the questions he grapples with. Racked by physical and emotional pain, he seeks help from all quarters: doctors, sex therapists, magicians, prostitutes, and fellow snake charmers. Bombarded with facts and ideas that leave his head spinning and his heart aching, Sonalal must sift through the "science" to find his own truth. Why do we destroy the things we love? What is real and what is magic? And, in the end, what does any of it mean? Sonalal's perfect, fleeting moment, and its devastating, all-too-human end, catapult him to a level of consciousness few of us have the courage to withstand. His heroic, painful attempts to divine life's greatest mysteries leave us wondering if he wouldn't have been better off never having experienced "the ether that flows through the universe." But it also leaves us, like Sonalal, grappling with questions as universal and unanswerable as those posed in the song of Kabir that Reena sings to him:

> *From which place did you come?*
> *And to which shore do you fly?*
> *Where will you stop to rest?*
> *And what are you looking for?*

ABOUT SANJAY NIGAM

Sanjay Nigam was born in India, but left as an infant when his father came to North America for postdoctoral studies. Although he spent most of his young life in Arizona, he regularly returned to India to visit his grandparents in Delhi, where *The Snake Charmer,* his first novel, is set. Nigam's colorful depictions of Old Delhi are derived from those childhood memories. While pursuing his medical training, Nigam found respite from his grueling medical residency in the world of literature. Eventually, his passion for reading led to his own fiction, which he began to work on while doing scientific research in New York City. There he became involved in writing workshops, and published his first short story—an excerpt from *The Snake Charmer*—in the prestigious literary magazine *Grand Street*. He has published other works in *The Kenyon Review, Story,* and *Natural History.* Sanjay Nigam has lived on both coasts and been associated with a number of prestigious medical schools, including Harvard.

A Conversation with Sanjay Nigam

Where did you come up with the idea for such an unusual opening?

There was a news story a few years back about a villager bit by a snake who, in anger, bit it back. Since I wrote this book, several have told me stories of people bitten by snakes who've bitten them back. Either this is not as unusual as I first thought, or I've started something.

Why a snake charmer?

Given the news story, it was an obvious choice. But at the time, I felt challenged by the problem of putting a name, face, and life on what is an exotic cliché. In some ways, it began as an attempt to bust the cliché, but soon I became much more interested in Sonalal as a character and forgot my agenda. Rather than busting the cliché, I began having fun with it. Hopefully, I haven't helped to perpetuate it.

Sonalal and his sons seem to represent a clashing of generations in India. Whereas Sonalal may never really have had a chance to improve his standing in life, his sons are clearly less limited. Have you witnessed this kind of change in India?

Although India remains heavily bound by tradition, especially in rural areas, in the cities there is the potential to escape tradition. Radical upward mobility may be rare, but at least it's a possibility in places like Bombay and Delhi, where the novel is set.

There's something very magical about the way Sonalal is introduced to the world of science. Even though he finds that facts "rob the world of its poetry," the information he receives from Dr. Seth is filled with metaphor and imagery. Do you see the "poetry" in science during your work?

Not nearly enough. The rigor and tediousness of daily scientific work—not to mention what is sometimes an obsession with what might seem a minor point but could make or break a whole argument (and often does)—makes it difficult to perceive the poetry. It's mainly when I'm thinking broadly or I'm away from it all that I appreciate the connections: the poetry. There's lots, if one takes the time to look.

What about Kekule's dream? The image of a snake biting its own tail is one of the central metaphors of the book.

One of them. I enjoyed connecting the image of the snake biting its tail to the cosmic ether, the aromas of spicy appetizers, and—need I say?—mangoes. I was surprised how far all that could go. And then Sonalal's own story is a bit like a snake biting its own tail. But the image of the bisected Raju, Sonalal's efforts to put him back together—resurrect his beloved companion—and his lifelong quest to come to terms with the fact that he cannot, echoes the Partition of India in 1947 (into what are now India, Pakistan, and Bangladesh) and its consequences.

Many times in the novel, Sonalal seems on the verge of partially redeeming himself, but it never quite happens. Hope is balanced against Sonalal's accumulated guilt. Even the final paragraph is like that.

I guess I see Sonalal trapped in a maze of impossibilities: the impossibility of redemption, the impossibility of producing sublime art, the impossibility of making sense of human existence and its vicissitudes, the impossibility of fulfilling love, the impossibility of a happy family life. But, though trapped in that maze, Sonalal tries like hell to find his way out. And every time he fails, he does his best to comprehend his predicament. And then, if there's a way, he tries again. That's why, despite his considerable flaws, despite his periodic obtuseness, I think there's something hopeful, and even heroic, in Sonalal's struggles.

As an Indian man immersed in Western culture, how does your ethnicity affect the way you live your life in America? Can you "take India out of the man" or are you constantly reminded of your ancestry?

I'm not "constantly reminded" of my ancestry, but as a writer, I'm certainly conscious of it. At least on the outside, I'm what people might call "assimilated," though I'm not sure a visible minority can ever feel completely invisible. But that's beside the point. In my case, the question isn't one of taking India out of the man, but of making room for both America and India in the man and seeing what emerges.

You have stated that you turned to writing fiction as both an antidote to the "realities" of the medical profession and as a way of dealing with the intensity of life as a medical resident. Still, it's unusual to find an individual who is able to thrive in both arenas. How do you account for your success in the worlds of science and literature?

Is it that unusual, though? There is definitely a long tradition of doctor-writer "types." A number of contemporary examples come to mind, and everyone knows about Chekov, Céline, William Carlos Williams, and so on. The question is why. I believe it arises, in part, out of a kind of double vision of life as it should be—normal, healthy—and life as it is in ICUs and ERs, where, of course, one is struck by how vulnerable and fragile the whole thing is. Health and disease, normal and pathological, life as it should be and life as it is. That is the constant preoccupation of the doctor, and I think this very existential tension helps turn some of them into writers.

You've mentioned that when you started reading as a doctor-in-training, you took on literature that was "heavy," such as Tolstoy, Dostoyevsky, and Gabriel García Márquez. With these substantial works as an introduction to the world of fiction, how do you account for the relative brevity of your own novel?

Ultimately, length should be dictated by the needs of the story you want to tell. Sonalal is preoccupied by the "big questions," but I believed the tale I wanted to tell was best rendered in a shorter work. Maybe the next book will be longer.

QUESTIONS FOR DISCUSSION

1) Why does Sonalal kill the snake? Aside from being angry that the snake has bitten him, what else is going on in this scene that might account for Sonalal's extreme rage? What do we learn later about Sonalal's relationship with his biological sons, and about the extent of his happiness with Raju, that might explain the action?

2) Nigam returns again and again to the moment when Sonalal bit Raju. How does that single incident—and the events leading up to it—shape the novel itself?

3) How would you account for the various maladies visited on Sonalal after Raju's death? Are they coincidental or triggered by the guilt he feels about killing Raju? Does he deserve this fate? Do you think he should have tried harder to redeem himself through his own actions rather than through the healing suggestions of various doctors?

4) What can science do for a man like Sonalal, who is illiterate, poor, and ignorant? Would education make him happier, or would it merely "rob the world of its poetry"?

5) What does Sonalal really learn from his encounters with Dr. Seth and Dr. Basu? How do both doctors hinder—and help—him in his efforts to relieve his suffering?

6) Although the novel is chiefly about Sonalal, Nigam creates a number of strong and quirky characters. How do Sonalal's interactions with each of these characters propel him along? What do the consequences of these interactions reveal about Sonalal?

7) What do you think of Sarita, Sonalal's wife? Is she really just a shrew with no compassion for her husband, or does she have a right to be

impatient with his apparent lack of ambition, his disregard for his sons, and his lack of feeling for her? What do you think accounts for the times, rare as they may be, when the couple seems to be getting along?

8) What aspects of Sonalal's story and character strike you as being distinctly Indian? How does Nigam infuse the novel with Western overtones? If Sonalal were a character in a novel that took place in America, what do you think would be his occupation? What sorts of doctors would he visit to heal himself? How might his story have ended differently—or would his fate resemble Sonalal's?

9) How does magic figure in this novel? Do we—or Sonalal—witness any true feats of magic? How does Jagat define magic when he comments to Sonalal that "Maya's veil isn't over the world, it's over their eyes. Your eyes! You must lift the veil, Sona—see the way you used to"?

10) Why do you think Sonalal is able to find such happiness with Reena? What does she give him that Sarita cannot? What happens during their weeklong vacation that changes Sonalal's outlook on life and his feelings for her?

11) Why do you think Sonalal is so drawn to Dr. Seth? Even though the doctor makes all sorts of distasteful and strange suggestions about what may be causing Sonalal's ailments, Sonalal continues to seek him out, even in prison. What does Sonalal learn from the doctor? Is he really a quack? What does Dr. Seth's prescriptive potpourri of psychology, philosophy, and holistic medicine say about how we can heal ourselves?

12) How does Sonalal's search for redemption and relief from his emotional and physical ailments reflect the encroachment of Western ideas and practices into traditional Indian culture?

For information about other Penguin Readers Guides,
please call the Penguin Marketing Department at (800) 778-6425,
email at reading@penguinputnam.com, or write to us at:

Penguin Marketing Department CC
Readers Guides
375 Hudson Street
New York, NY 10014-3657

Please allow 4–6 weeks for delivery.

To access Penguin Readers Guides on-line, visit Club PPI on our
Web site at: http//www.penguinputnam.com.

FOR THE BEST IN PAPERBACKS, LOOK FOR THE

In every corner of the world, on every subject under the sun, Penguin represents quality and variety—the very best in publishing today.

For complete information about books available from Penguin—including Puffins, Penguin Classics, and Arkana—and how to order them, write to us at the appropriate address below. Please note that for copyright reasons the selection of books varies from country to country.

In the United Kingdom: Please write to *Dept. EP, Penguin Books Ltd, Bath Road, Harmondsworth, West Drayton, Middlesex UB7 0DA.*

In the United States: Please write to *Penguin Putnam Inc., P.O. Box 12289 Dept. B, Newark, New Jersey 07101-5289* or call *1-800-788-6262.*

In Canada: Please write to *Penguin Books Canada Ltd, 10 Alcorn Avenue, Suite 300, Toronto, Ontario M4V 3B2.*

In Australia: Please write to *Penguin Books Australia Ltd, P.O. Box 257, Ringwood, Victoria 3134.*

In New Zealand: Please write to *Penguin Books (NZ) Ltd, Private Bag 102902, North Shore Mail Centre, Auckland 10.*

In India: Please write to *Penguin Books India Pvt Ltd, 11 Panchsheel Shopping Centre, Panchsheel Park, New Delhi 110 017.*

In the Netherlands: Please write to *Penguin Books Netherlands bv, Postbus 3507, NL-1001 AH Amsterdam.*

In Germany: Please write to *Penguin Books Deutschland GmbH, Metzlerstrasse 26, 60594 Frankfurt am Main.*

In Spain: Please write to *Penguin Books S. A., Bravo Murillo 19, 1° B, 28015 Madrid.*

In Italy: Please write to *Penguin Italia s.r.l., Via Benedetto Croce 2, 20094 Corsico, Milano.*

In France: Please write to *Penguin France, Le Carré Wilson, 62 rue Benjamin Baillaud, 31500 Toulouse.*

In Japan: Please write to *Penguin Books Japan Ltd, Kaneko Building, 2-3-25 Koraku, Bunkyo-Ku, Tokyo 112.*

In South Africa: Please write to *Penguin Books South Africa (Pty) Ltd, Private Bag X14, Parkview, 2122 Johannesburg.*